The SEARCH *for*
REATH

D.L. CRAWFORD

The SEARCH for REATH

A Whimsically Long Short Story

Illustrated by Maia Jenkins

XULON PRESS

Xulon Press
2301 Lucien Way #415
Maitland, FL 32751
407.339.4217

www.xulonpress.com

© 2020 by D.L. Crawford

Printed in the United States of America.

ISBN-13: 978-1-6305-0248-5

For Leigh, Julia, Charlotte, and Will

The Contents, in Table Form

The Introduction

NOT TOO LONG AGO, ABOUT A DREAM-AND-A-half away from where you live, there was a land called Aponna.[1] The residents of this land just happened to be talking animals.

Talking animals? "But animals don't talk!" you might say. And you would be right. Except for parrots. But they don't really count, because parrots are just adapting by making sounds in an uncomprehending manner in order to join a clan, not really talking, per se...

Wait, I'm getting off the subject. Where was I? Oh yes—talking animals. The animals in this story *did* talk, and they were also quite intelligent— possibly more intelligent than some of the people you know.[2] And they

---

[1] This is pronounced uh-PAWN-uh. And if converting from metric units, it is closer to 1.75 dreams away.

[2] This is not to imply that your friends are unintelligent. Just that some of these animals are pretty smart, and there are certain scientific reports by Aponnan statisticians indicating probability in this area.

lived in a different world anyway, so the fact that they talked is not that strange after all, is it?

They worked. They played. They paid taxes. They had families, friends, and adventures. And they grew through challenges, trials, and victories.

In this land of Aponna, there was a group of villages aptly named the Cluster Villages. Our story begins in one of these villages—with a squirrel. And he is shooting arrows at a mouse.

The Chapter with Archery Practice

"**H**OLD STILL," SAID SEVERT[3] AS HE STEADIED his bow for a third shot.

Squirrels always tended to have the strongest sense of aim in Aponna, but Severt considered himself one of the best in the Arrant Archer-Knights regiment. Last time he had taken a survey of opinion, that had been the result, and Severt wasn't particularly concerned that no one else had been in attendance at that meeting

"I'm just...I'm just...slightly nervous, you know... and..." muttered the mouse, who was the one who was supposed to hold still.

"Now, my dear Freightfurt," interrupted Severt in his most noble tone of voice. "Have not my thrice previous efforts flown true?"

---

[3]   The name of our squirrel friend is actually pronounced "Suh-VARE." Sort of a French thing. His parents probably meant it to be pronounced "See-vert," but he's just a little pretentious. Or I am. Anyway. Carry on.

The nervous mouse glanced down at the three fruits lying on the ground beside him with arrows protruding from their centers. "Sure. They were...pretty true, I suppose."

"It's just that I was wondering," Freightfurt continued, "why this exercise is necessary. Don't get me wrong, it's always a pleasure to witness your skills with the bow..."

"And a pleasure to be witnessed," Severt said, tipping his hat.

"But the wolves have not attacked the villages in years, and I think they are...pretty much keeping to themselves these days."

"*Keeping to themselves*?" Severt said, suddenly taken aback. "Keeping to themselves? Is that what wolves do now—keep to themselves? I suppose they will also polish your watch and serve you tea and biscuits."

Severt also considered himself one of the best at formulating sarcastic zingers. This had been decided at the same meeting as the archery assessment.

"Well..." Freightfurt started, "Not tea exactly. They are partial to room-temperature beverages, I hear..."

"The wolves will *not* keep to themselves! Not as long as they sense fear," Severt exclaimed, curling his gloved hand into a fist. "And as long as we keep ourselves at the ready, we shall give them *nothing* to sense."

"Eloquently said...sir." Freightfurt nodded slightly, accidentally sending the current fruit, which had been atop his head, falling to the ground. He quickly extended his paw and caught it on the way down. He surprised himself with the sudden catch and looked up to Severt for approval.

But Severt was looking elsewhere.

A young lady fox with a red robe that Severt had noticed several times in town recently had emerged from the trees and was crossing the clearing several yards away. She was carrying a bundle of something they couldn't quite make out.

Severt was often distracted when she walked by during his exercises. He hoped she would notice his prowess, but she never threw him a second look. Or a first, really.

"A finer beauty I have never witnessed. A vision, truly," Severt said to himself, entranced.

"And...exercises concluded," Freightfurt said with some degree of relief. The lady fox had provided an opening that allowed Freightfurt to stop being shot at, and he was grateful. He took a bite from the fruit he had caught so impressively.

Meanwhile, Severt was closing the gap in pursuit of his canine interest. "Miss!" Severt called aloud while crossing the road, slinging his bow across his shoulder. "Miss! Can I help you with your burden?"

The lady fox looked over her shoulder, noticing Severt for the first time.

"Me?" the girl asked, quickening her pace. "I am quite alright, actually. Just taking some items to market. It's no matter, really."

"Come now," said a persistent Severt. "What goodly knight of the Arrant regiment would see a lady under weight of load and then not offer to lift in relief?"

"Okay…you're goodly, I get it, you're goodly. But *I'm* good. Gotta go," she said and then doubled her pace in such a manner that even our protagonist squirrel would not miss the hint. She sped off into the town with her bundle wrapped tightly under her arm.

Severt halted his progress and stood in place staring at the ground, ruminating. "That is *quite* surprising…." Severt said aloud to himself.

Freightfurt observed this with the empathy that only a kind mouse, who had just recently been shot at by his target of concern, would allow.

"I wouldn't let it get to you…" Freightfurt muttered over a mouthful of fruit.

"Indeed…quite surprising." Severt lifted his head. "*So* surprising that she cannot contain her obvious affection for a handsome, noble archer-knight such as myself!"

Yep, he can miss the hint alright, Freightfurt thought to himself.

"No point in following her at this point in time, I suppose," Severt said, striding back toward the mouse.

5

"Freightfurt, reset the fresh target. Time to resume our exercise! Flow Recon is tomorrow, and we can't be caught short in the skills department!"

"Er, I kind of just…ate..the target," said Freightfurt, holding up the half-eaten rind.

"Ah, it appears to be so," Severt agreed. He slung the bow back over his shoulder. "Well, tarry here for the next hour or so, my good assistant. I shall go and attain new targets! Now, where shall I find more fruit for target practice…?"

"There are some nice trees over there…" Freightfurt started to say.

"Ah! I know where to find more," Severt interrupted, winking at Freightfurt. "At the marketplace, of course."

Severt then set off in the direction of the same market square destination previously specified by the lady fox.

"Nope, he did *not* get the hint." Freightfurt sighed and took another bite.

The Chapter with the Drawings

S HADMACK SET DOWN HIS LANTERN AND nibbled a bit on his claws. He always did so with nervous excitement when he was on the brink of a big discovery.

And this one was a *doozy*—if it was, in fact, what he *thought* it was.

The badger reached up and brushed away a bit more dirt from the etchings on the ancient wall. He was standing in the remains of an ancient Aponnan building. It had just been discovered by the AHS[4] the month previously, and these were the first interesting markings he had found. The light outside had faded with the setting sun. In order to see better, he had to light a second— then a third—extra lantern to shine enough light on his subject.

---

[4]   Aponnan Historical Society. Our badger friend here is the vice president, and very hands-on with the finds, due to a fairly small staff.

This cave wall was telling a story, and Shadmack was eager to listen.

Pictured on the stone wall was a round hole with what looked like several figures—animals of various species from several walks of life—falling into it. Below this was a landscape with large rectangles, wagons, and what seemed to be large ponds. Set around these ponds were objects that looked like glowing stones or gems of some kind. The figures were seen walking along the edges of the ponds, gathering these gems, and then walking back up through a very similar hole holding these treasures.

The implication was pure, and the meaning obvious; he was looking at a depiction of the legendary land of Reath. The gems carried by the figures depicted in the illustration, according to ancient Reath myths, were probably "Reathstones."

Reath: The Land of Untold Riches. Now "told," of course...at least in cave wall form. The Reathstones were a means of passage into Reath, but exactly *how* continued to elude Shadmack.

He was thrilled for the time being, however, because at least now he had a *map* of where the legendary world might be located.

He leaned in close to inspect the first circle—the one that the journeying animals had first entered to reach Reath. There were some triangles around it, as well as what looked like a spinning top of some sort.

Let's see, thought Shadmack. *Based on the geography depicted, with the lake here and the triangles—probably trees—here, it looks like the location is...*

He sat back and drew a sigh of disappointment. It looked like the entrance to Reath was in the worst sort of location: the Blue Mountains.

Dangerously close to Flow Country.

The Flow, you see, lived in the north across the lake from the Five Villages. They were wolves, but *not* your typical good-natured type of wolf. Oh, no.[5] Flow wolves were a particularly nasty type of wolf and had threatened the Cluster Villages with harm numerous times in the past.

He had hoped that the entrance to Reath would have been somewhere somewhat more pleasant. Somewhere he wouldn't be somewhat captured or, worse, somewhat eaten. It was clear that he was going to have to employ more help. This meant splitting whatever treasure he was able to find.

That's okay, Shadmack thought. *I am motivated by Knowledge and Historical Discovery*, he told himself, *not Being Rich*. He rather prided himself on being that way.

For help in this investigation, he'd need someone interested in Untold Riches who didn't mind some degree of danger.

Fortunately, he knew just the right person.

---

[5] Quite the opposite, as you could probably tell from their name.

The Chapter with the Cube

JOSLYN TOOK A COUPLE OF STEPS ACROSS THE rock bridge spanning a deep hole in the cave. A chunk of rock chipped off and fell into the deep chasm below her. Luckily for her, felines can keep their balance in moments such as these. And panthers with her amount of experience? Even more so.

She reached the other side and then hurriedly had to duck as a giant circular boulder shot out from the cave wall. Someone less skilled would be missing a head at this point, a considerable inconvenience since most persons typically possess only one.

Trap #1: Done, she thought.

She scanned across the new room she found herself in. There were thick vines that had grown across the opposite wall. But instead of growing directly up like most vines — and plants in general — do, they had grown diagonally and upward to the right.

Sunlight, she thought to herself. *They are growing toward sunlight.* She knew that she should avoid that direction because traps could often be set off by breaking beams of sunlight. Or so she had learned from previous close calls.

Joslyn searched the ground at her feet, trying to find something substantial enough that it could block out a beam of sunlight. She quickly located a small fist-sized bag of sand lying on the ground. *Probably from a previous adventurer,* she thought to herself.

She slowly leaned over to look around the corner and saw dust dancing in a line of sunlight.

There you are, she said to herself and tossed the sand toward the light.

As soon as the sack of sand entered the area of sunbeam, the floor disappeared! Or, rather, it just folded in on itself. Anyone standing on it at that moment would have been swallowed by the mass of rock. However, in this case, it created a stone bridge that she could now walk across.

Trap #2: Done.

She started to inch her way across the bridge, darkness yawning below her on either side. Joslyn made a mental note to add 'tight wire acts across narrow bridges of stone' to her resume.

But something didn't feel right. She stepped back off the bridge and turned around 180 degrees. She stared at the rock wall next to the area she had just come from. Very uninteresting patterns were on the wall there, nothing more. Nondescript, so as not to draw attention. And obviously designed to be that way, which is why they drew Joslyn's attention.

She walked over to get a closer look and noticed a small square that seemed a little out of place. *Nondescript* and out of place.

She traced the square pattern with her finger. As she traced the pattern, she noticed that it was loosening and a square section of the wall was about to fall out. As soon as she completed the square, the whole square chunk fell to the ground, creating a hole in its place. She reached in through the square hole to find what felt like a latch of some sort.

I've come this far; might as well chance it, she thought to herself. She pulled up on the latch and braced herself for horrible things. But horrible things didn't happen. Instead, the whole wall sank into the floor to reveal a small six-foot-by-six-foot chamber. In the middle of it sat a dais, and on the dais sat a box.

She walked up to the dais, looking at the ceiling and walls, trying to find what sort of trap could be here. Nothing looked untoward. But just to be safe...

She quickly lunged across the room, sailing through the air. She snatched the box off the podium in mid-flight and landed with a somersault on the opposite side, just as the floor—in similar fashion to the neighboring area she had just arrived from—folded up and disappeared, leaving yet another small shelf of rock, or "bridge," in its place.

Trap #3? Done!

She examined the box, a stone cube of sorts, and the ornate symbols scratched on its surface. She anticipated what might be inside. Ancient tablets? Gold? Sapphires? Bracelets?

She turned it over several times in her hands, trying to find a clasp or button of some kind with which to open the enigmatic find. None could be found.

"Doesn't look like much," Joslyn muttered. "I just hope I still get paid."

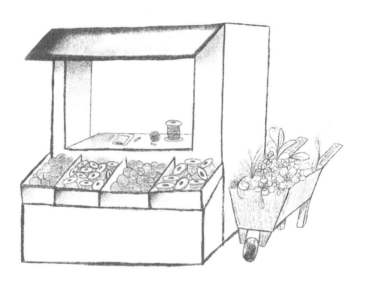

The Chapter with the Market

S EVERT HAD ONLY SEEN THE YOUNG LADY FOX a couple of times in the last couple of weeks. And probably a couple of times before that. But he was already quite smitten. Severt guessed that she was from a neighboring village, different from his home village of Arrant. It was strange that she would come to the market in Arrant, when the other four villages in the Cluster had their own burgeoning markets. But one shouldn't underestimate the charms of Arrant. Or of its Archer-Knights.

He strode into the bustling marketplace and surveyed the surrounding area. Dozens of carts in dozens of rows stood with everything from rice and potatoes to papyrus and bells. An open market was held every week, but the mega-market was only once a month, so today was a very special day for many of these merchants, who would be seeking over half of their monthly income in one afternoon.

He walked past a few booths. One was selling threads. Exceedingly large spools of thread.

"Thread for you, sir?" said the merchant, an armadillo with a fake-looking moustache.

"No thanks," said the squirrel archer.

"You never know when you might need them!"

Severt ignored this appeal, and several others similar to it, as he rounded the corner and spotted the object of his search. Her red robe was unmistakable as she leaned over the counter to speak to the handsome male feline merchant there. Apparently he was a seller of cloth of some sort, but Severt was more focused on the possibility of rivalry. She finished her covert conversation with the merchant and had turned to leave when she spotted Severt.

"Madam," Severt said. "How pleasant to run into you again! It is indeed a small village after all. What are the odds?"

"Oh," she said, startled. "The archer." She shrugged awkwardly, not sure what to follow "oh, the archer" with. She settled on: "You really shouldn't be practicing archery here; it could be somewhat dangerous with so many people around."

Severt removed his cap. "And yet *you* persist," he said. "For here I stand, pierced through the heart."

He bowed his head and extended his paw. He stood like that a few moments and then looked up because she had not taken it. In fact, she had taken leave. Completely.

"Can I at least know your name?" Severt exclaimed as she hurriedly walked away.

The young fox was not responding to his advances. *Too shy, perhaps*, he thought. He turned to the vendor that she had been conversing with—the one that was handsome, but not as handsome as Severt, of course (and surely the unnamed red-robed maiden had noticed this fact as well).

"Dear Sir Merchant..." Severt said to him, causing him to look up from sorting his wares.

"It's 'George,'" the merchant interrupted.

"...Sir George, then... Can you tell me the name of your client?"

"Which client do you mean?"

"The lady fox. The one with the red robe," he clarified.

"Oh, that one. Yes, she goes by the name of Meryam. She's from another Cluster village. Erramore, I think. That's all I know really."

"Meryam... Of course she would have a lovely name to match the face," Severt said to himself.

Severt turned to address the merchant directly. "I trust you would not be an adversary for her affections?"

"Of course not." The merchant shrugged. "I'm a happily married man."

Severt breathed out a sigh. Not a sigh of *relief*—oh, no. The Champion in Charm was never in question. He was merely relieved this good man was spared heartbreak.

"Very good. Well, I shall take my leave, then," Severt said and turned to go.

"Er, one more thing, Mr. Knight," said the merchant.

"Yes?"

The merchant leaned in close to whisper. "I think I'd take it down a notch." He nodded his head in the direction of the departed girl.

Severt thought about this a moment. Then he reached up to the strap that secured the quiver of arrows around his shoulder. He unfastened the clasp and loosened it, letting out some slack in the strap. Then he re-clasped it and gave it a tug.

"Ah! Much more comfortable. Clearly you are an expert in your trade!" Severt flipped the merchant a coin and strode away.

Watching him leave, the merchant pocketed the coin.

Poor guy has no clue, he thought, before turning to engage another customer.

The Chapter with the Evil

S ARNAL PULLED THE LAST BONE OF THE RABBIT between his teeth and chewed the last bit of meat. He was not particularly fond of rabbit, but that was all nature had offered him today. Food variety was harder to come by in the mountains of Flow; the best game had already been hunted and eaten. They needed to expand their territory, and soon. The best game was across the lake in the Cluster Villages; but the time had not yet come to lay claim to that territory. Not yet.

It was good to let Aponna, and the Aponnans that infested the land there, *think* the Flow had lost interest in that piece of the world. Let them live in that delusion for a little longer. Soon the wolves of Flow, led by Sarnal himself, would reunite with their lost brothers and take what rightfully belonged to them.

Many years had passed since the incident at the Bent Tree Clearing.

It was an Ancient Place. A place the wolves had not heard of, even though it lay near the heart of their land. It had taken an adventuring party of animals – seeking treasure and history – to reveal its location.

Sarnal still did not know the complete story, or what was supposed to be on the Other Side, but he intended to find out. And when he did, he would retrieve his army – and his own brother – in the process.

With his leadership skills, and his brother's army, they would lay waste to the Villages that rightfully belonged to him.

Sarnal made a sour face and spit out the last bit of rabbit meat.

Soon.

The Chapter with the Map Discovery

SHADMACK PUT DOWN HIS PEN AND EXAMINED his register.

14000 Leafs[6]! He thought to himself. 14000! The museum would only be able to operate for three months at that amount. Barely two, even. The Society's accounting woes were getting out of hand. Since the latest round of artifacts had been displayed many moons ago, the frequency of visitors had slowed to a crawl. They needed a refresh, and soon. The upcoming Arts and History Festival would generate some funds, but they needed something to show there in order to promote the museum.

Shadmack loved the historian part of his job. He did not particularly like the business end of it.

---

[6] Leafs are the currency of the Cluster Villages. Not to be confused with "leaves," of course. Making currency out of actual leaves could cause all sorts of problems with exchange rates and would be a real nightmare for accountants.

It was past time for Joslyn to bring in some more items for the museum. Yes, *that* Joslyn: our panther character from a few pages back. She was a frequent associate of Shadmack's and would often travel to distant corners of the land, bringing back baubles, trinkets, and knickknacks. But supply had dried up as of late.

A knock came on the door, and Shadmack went to answer it. "Who's there?" said Shadmack as he approached.

"Me," said Joslyn from the other side of the door.

Speak of the devil, thought Shadmack. He knew she had been on a mission. Perhaps she had retrieved a new artifact or two for the festival.

"Please come in and have a seat," Shadmack said, opening the door.

"I know this will surprise you," the lady panther said, sitting down. "But that cavern in the Eastern Highlands did not have any ancient Flow statues in it."

Shadmack took a seat at his desk across from Joslyn. On the desk were strewn several items he had been working on, including a rubbing[7] of the Reath map from his earlier dig.

"Sorry to hear." He sighed. "Of course, the Foundation will compensate you for your time."

"What do you want with Flow artifacts anyway?" Joslyn asked, grabbing a piece of fruit from a bowl on the table between them and taking a bite. "Those

---

[7] Rubbing is something historians do to transfer images on cave walls to paper. Don't try it without proper training; you'll just make a mess.

wolves aren't exactly going to be thrilled if they find out we're putting pieces of their ancient culture – if you even want to call it 'culture' – on display."

"I doubt that." Shadmack shrugged. "There are not that many Flow wolves around anymore, and they probably have less interest in their own culture than most Aponnans nowadays."

"Don't take this the wrong way, Mack," Joslyn leaned forward, "but this isn't the first time you've suggested some out-of-the-way site to find treasure. And then when I get there...no treasure."

"Joslyn, in all the years I've employed you as an, er, 'requisitioner' of fine things, have I ever asked you to explore anything that turned out to be a non-starter?"

Joslyn thought a moment. "Well, there was that time with the Crystal Ball, which ended up just being a shiny coconut."

"Yes, there was that," Shadmack admitted.

"Oh, and there was also the Perplexing Pickle of Pulchritudinous Platitudes, which ended up just being a load of meaningless nonsense.[8]

"And that time you had me climb the Mysterious Memory Tree."

"I don't remember much about that one exactly..." Shadmack thought aloud.

"I don't either. But that's beside the point! The point is...I'm tired of quests that just end up as dead ends. You don't have a lot of money, the museum doesn't

---

[8] Kind of like that sentence.

have a lot of money, and I can't make a living off of ancient cubes."

Shadmack looked up. "Ancient what?"

"This." Joslyn tossed the cube she found from the cavern onto Shadmack's desk. "A cube of some sort. Meant to mention it earlier."

He lifted it off his desk and examined it.

"Hmm....looks like pre-Arraponnan Era. Could use more bone in the composition, I suppose, to be sure. But I would have to do a thorough cleaning to determine that. Also, although the lack of inscription would seem to indicate a post-Erelean context..."

"Is it worth anything, Mack?" Joslyn interrupted.

Shadmack glanced up at her. "Without further study I can't really be sure. Did you figure out how to open it?"

"No. That's why you get paid the big leafs instead of me, Doc," Joslyn said. "Ever try to open an Ancient Cube that has no buttons, clasps, or instructions of any kind? Me neither."

Shadmack stared at the cube for a few moments, mental gears working furiously.

"I suppose we could throw it at the wall and see what happens," Joslyn suggested.

Shadmack shuddered. "This type of material composition is too strong. Also, really? Destroy an ancient artifact that might...?"

Shadmack trailed off as he looked at the parchment where he had placed the cube. He just happened to have set it next to the curious illustration of the triangles with the spinning top that had perplexed him earlier. "Maybe not *throw* it. But perhaps, *spin* it..." he conjectured.

Shadmack took the cube and placed it on his desk, balancing it on one corner, and gave it a slight spin.

Even though it was just a slight spin, it picked up quite a bit of speed, as if it was spinning itself!

Then, suddenly, it stopped and unfolded neatly on the desk. Upon opening, four stones spilled out of it, as well as a bunch of sand that had prevented them from rattling inside it prior to opening.

Shadmack and Joslyn looked at each other and then back down to the newly opened cube and the rocks.

"Well, it isn't treasure exactly...but I *am* intrigued," Joslyn said.

Shadmack examined the rocks. "These do seem to be just plain rock—granite or igneous of some sort, I believe. But they appear to have letters carved into them," Shadmack said, examining one. "Look."

Joslyn looked closer. "I see. Yes, this one has a small letter 'A.' That one has a 'T.'"

"And 'E,' and 'H' on these," Shadmack observed.

"Maybe they are supposed to spell something..." Shadmack thought aloud, looking again at the same tablet he had been examining earlier and where he had gathered the clue on how to spin open the cube.

He re-arranged the letters in a couple of configurations on the table.

Hmm, he thought.

"Care to clue me in, Mack?" asked Joslyn.

29

"Well, it could be a coincidence, I suppose...however unlikely." He looked up at Joslyn. "This may have something to do with Reath."

"Who is 'Reath'?" Joslyn asked. "Someone you know?"

"It's not a person; it's a place."

"Don't think I've ever been there," Joslyn said.

"Not many have, if any at all. It's a mythical place with not much written about it. It's mostly used to entertain kids when they are young and then scare them when they are adults."

"It was visited many years ago, so the stories go," Shadmack continued, "by a group of Flow and Aponnans who never returned, and it's unclear what happened to them exactly. Perhaps they could not find their way back. Or maybe they liked it there and wanted to stay. And they might have *wanted* to stay because it is said to be a land of Untold Riches."

"Stop," Joslyn said, throwing up a paw. "You had me at 'Untold Riches.'"

"But that was literally at the end of everything I said..." Shadmack said.

"Got it," Joslyn exclaimed jumping up from her chair. "So, how do we get there?"

"Well, that's the trick, isn't it? Granted, I've done a lot of reading over the years about Reath and probably know as much or more about the subject as anyone in the Cluster."

"If I didn't respect your work," Joslyn offered, "I wouldn't keep working for you."

"Very kind of you," he responded. "The problem, though, is that a lot of what was written about Reath often seems contradictory or ends up being about something or somewhere else entirely. I'm afraid some of your missions that have resulted in dead ends were related to those misleading clues."

"I see," said Joslyn. "So, let's get back to how you think we can get to the Untold Rich...er, I mean, Reath."

"Well, you're not going to like the location; it's in the Blue Mountains."

"Flow Territory?"

"Close to Flow Territory."

"*Dangerously* close, I'd say," Joslyn said. "But, of course, the Flow are practically a myth themselves lately. Nobody's heard from them in a very long time."

"The other problem is these stones," Shadmack said, indicating their discovery on the desk. "We're missing the letter 'R.' And I could be mistaken that these others are Reathstones at all."

"'Reathstones?'"

"Yes—a group of stones that acted as a sort of key that allowed you to transition to the 'Other World,' the 'Reath World,' etc. There were all sorts of names for Reath. Some even just called it the 'Land of Change.'"

"Well, *these* stones obviously don't spell out 'Change.'" Joslyn stood up. "But considering how little 'change' I have in my pockets nowadays, I'm up for seeing if they spell 'Reath.'"

"So, shall we venture north? Say, tomorrow after breakfast?"

They shook paws.

The Chapter with the Recon

DAWN HAD COME THIS MORNING IN A VERY sneaky fashion. Ever notice how some days the sun just blazes up into the sky with fanfare, but then with others it can sometimes gradually fade in after a cloudy morning? Totally black one minute, dark gray the next, then several shades of gray until there comes a time when you can comfortably assert it is daytime, even though the sun is still stubbornly staying behind a layer of cloud.

Freightfurt wished it would be full-on day already. He was not particularly fond of their mission today, and he needed all the cheery sun he could get.

"Recon Day is *not* my favorite." Freightfurt shuddered as he and Severt walked along the side of the Lake. On their west were the Blue Mountains, and further north from them was the part of the Mountains that was in Flow Territory. If Flow still actually lived there, of course. They had not been seen in many a moon.

"Don't worry, my good Freightfurt. We aren't going all the way into the mountains. We just need to survey their activity. And, of course, see if they are amassing any forces at all."

Freightfurt nibbled the tip of his tail. He couldn't help but feel this was all a little too dangerous.

"They are still low in number," Freightfurt said, a note of optimism trying desperately to fight its way into his voice. "All the reports indicate that."

"And missions like ours today will either continue to bear that out..." Severt tugged on his quiver's strap, "...or tell a different story."

They continued their journey through more forest, the ground becoming more sloped and difficult to traverse. After a while, climbing up the gradual incline was becoming somewhat exhausting to Freightfurt, who had decided that he would suggest a brief respite.

All of a sudden, Severt placed a hand on Freightfurt's shoulder. "There," he said. "Do you see that?"

Freightfurt squinted into the distance and found what appeared to be a person clothed in black – or rather, the shadows likely just seemed to make them seem clothed in black – further up the hill in the trees.

"I wonder who it might be," Severt said to himself. "Quickly, let's get a closer look."

Walking up a steep incline of rough, uneven ground trying to dodge trees is a difficult task. Running up a steep incline of rough, uneven ground trying to dodge trees is just about impossible for an out-of-shape mouse.

Freightfurt was fairly certain that he was not going to make it to the figure before he completely passed out.

"Ahoy there!" Severt suddenly called in a loud whisper.

"Shhhhhh!" shushed the figure in the dark robe – or rather, a dark *red* robe, made darker by the shadow of the trees. As she turned to look back at the two of them, Severt immediately recognized the face in the hood: Meryam, the beautiful clothing enthusiast! "Stay back and don't be seen!" the lovely face warned.

She took another look at him. "Wait. Are you the archer? From the village? What are you doing here?" she whisper-shouted across the gap of many yards between them.

"The name is Severt," he responded. "And I should ask the same of you. A lovely lady such as yourself should not be alone in the Blue Mountains! Let me provide escort immediately."

"Thank you for the concern, Sir Knight, but I am on an...errand, currently...and it's very important that I do it alone."

Severt lowered his gaze slightly. "Would you perchance be seeking a rendezvous with that clothing merchant from the Arrant market? Is he coming here to meet you?" Severt asked, then straightened. "If so, I won't get in the way. He seems a good man."

"Who – George?" she asked. "That guy's married, for crying out loud! Look...I know you archer folks are all about protection. But I am going to be fine."

"Who are you meeting, then?" Severt said. "Someone friendly? Or someone dangerous, perhaps?"

His voice trailed off as they heard padding on the ground off to the right.

She glanced nervously in the direction of the footfalls. "That's them. Just...please, stay hidden!" she insisted and ran off with her basket into the clearing.

"An 'errand' in the Blue Mountains," Severt said in disbelief. "Who would do such a dangerous thing?"

"Us?" muttered Freightfurt.

Severt decided he was not going to leave until he was assured that she was safe. He walked through a patch of trees to regain a view of the lady fox and could not believe what he saw next.

Meryam was in the clearing talking to...a wolf!

A wolf indeed! Severt could see him now. Oh, the distress his damsel was in!

Severt quietly drew his sword and crouched in the bush with a near-fainting Freightfurt. While he was a skilled fighter, he knew there were likely other wolves in the forest as backup, and he would not be able to take on all of them alone. Severt would respect her wish to stay hidden, against his better instincts. But at the first sign of trouble, he would leap into action!

Severt and Freightfurt maneuvered quietly to a tree just within hearing to make out what was being said.

"I came. As the note instructed," she said. "Alone. And I have the item." She indicated the basket she carried.

"Yes, you have...Meryam, is it? Delightful name you chose there."

Severt, quietly sitting and listening in on the wolf and the girl's conversation, leaned over to Freightfurt and whispered, "Only a very precocious baby could choose their own name."

"Um, I think it's more like an alias she's using..."

"Shh!" Severt motioned. "She's showing him something."

Meryam pulled the blanket off of her package to reveal something in it to the wolf. They could not make out what was in the basket from their angle.

"I hope it's not her grandmother's cookies or something like that," Freightfurt asked. "Because that would *not* end well."

"I will need to be sure it works before I let you go," the wolf said to Meryam menacingly.

"It will work."

"We shall see. Please come with me." The wolf and the girl turned to walk further into the clearing.

Severt's restlessness had reached a fever pitch. He could not just sit and watch while this angel was led to her doom!

Curse that vile creature! He thought.

He turned to his companion. "Freightfurt, stay here."

"Good plan." Freightfurt nodded. "Will do."

Severt left the cover of the shrubs and quietly followed down the path.

There was the evil beast now. He might be able to get a clean shot, even at this distance. He quietly drew his bow and lined up an arrow; it was a finely crafted arrow he had just made last night after a delicious meal of corn cakes and root wine. He would have to have another glass tonight to celebrate this rescue. Perchance the lady would join him.

"I wouldn't do that if I were you!" the wolf suddenly growled over his shoulder.

Severt realized he had been discovered. He had tragically underestimated the wolf's powers of perception.

"Hold, you evil brute!" he called. "Release the maiden! She comes with me!"

The wolf stopped his tread and looked back at Severt. "I don't think so," he said calmly. "Instead, *you* will be coming with *us*."

Six other wolves stepped out of the woods, surrounding Severt. He loosened his grip on the bow.

"And so is your little friend."

Two wolves held up a bag with Freightfurt's head sticking out of the top. His eyes were wide open in fear, and a gag had been placed over his mouth.

Severt was not pleased with this setback, but he was determined to turn the situation around.

"Come. We have some work to do." The wolf grinned.

The Chapter with the Rhombus

JOSLYN AND SHADMACK ARRIVED AT THE clearing and looked at the strange shape formed by the trees on the opposite side. The group of trees on the left and the group of trees on the right curved toward each other as they reached the top of their canopy, forming a shape that was similar to the one pictured on Shadmack's rubbing. Then the trees behind them did the same thing, but they were shorter – as were the ones behind those – so as to create the illusion of a dark hole that receded in size toward the ground.

"This *does* look like the gateway to another world," Joslyn said. "Eerie, with very weird trees."

"My thought exactly," said Shadmack. "Now to determine how it works. Does one just walk through?"

"Yes. One does. Sort of." A deep voice said from behind them. Joslyn pulled her knife and spun around to address the owner of the deep voice.

A wolf. A rather large one.

Joslyn stood at the ready but then lowered her weapon as she noticed several other wolves revealing themselves in the forest around them. Joslyn and Shadmack came to the dismaying realization that they were now surrounded by Flow.

"Who are you?" she said to the wolf.

"I am a Flow," he said, circling them. "And you could say I *belong* here; this *is* Flow territory, after all."

"I believe current boundaries declare this area to be neutral," sputtered Shadmack. "At the moment. According to current documents and all."[9]

"Yes," said the wolf, pacing. "But it is *close,* isn't it? *Dangerously* close."

He paced a few more yards and said, "Consider me," he pointed one claw at himself, "to be your Guide through this dangerous area. I, Sarnal, will *guide* you to your destiny. And I will also guide your cohorts."

Out of the trees, some of the other wolves led some captives that had been tied at the wrists and gagged. One of them was a squirrel dressed in the garb of a soldier and wearing a bow and quiver. There was also a modestly-clad mouse and a fox lady in a red robe.

"Cohorts?" Joslyn said. "I've never seen them before in my life. Have you?" She looked over at Shadmack. He shook his head; he didn't know them either.

---

[9] According to conventional wisdom, it is best not to argue legal real estate boundaries with a threatening wolf. Regardless of whether he can talk or not.

"So, you don't know them? Doesn't matter," Sarnal said. "You can get to know each other on the Other Side."

He finished another circle around them and sat down halfway between them and the mysterious trees across from them.

He nodded in the direction of the bent trees and what looked like some rocks arranged in a square-ish shape in front of them. "Behold. The gateway to Reath. Some call it – what is the term – the Land of Untold Riches, I believe?"

Joslyn didn't particularly like the feel of this whole situation. What with the tied-up strangers, snarling wolves, and not being given a choice in the matter.

"If there *are* 'Untold Riches' in there.." Joslyn asked, looking sideways at Shadmack, "then why are you putting us in there, instead of going in yourself?"

Joslyn could tell by the concern on Shadmack's face that she wasn't going to like the answer.

"There's an expression," Sarnal said, "about *needing a 'Guinea Pig.'* I don't know where it comes from exactly. Maybe Guinea Pigs are particularly greedy, or courageous. Or neither. All I know is they are *scrumptious* when cooked in a fine broth."

Shadmack shuddered. Joslyn glowered.

"I need you to go through. And then I need to see if you can get back. You see, a similar band of adventurers tried this expedition many years ago and never came back. We think we might know why. Perhaps you will never come back. If you don't, I will…continue to not go through."

"Smart. Well, we were planning to go through anyway," said Joslyn. "But once we get through, maybe we'll like it there and want to stay…what then?"

"I doubt there is anything that would convince you to stay there. If so, then go ahead – stay. There are more where you came from – other villagers, such as your friends and family that you will have abandoned. I doubt it will come to that, however. There is too much on this side of the portal for you to walk away from."

He glared at the girl in the red robe. "Some of you more than others."

The wolves put away their knives. This could have been a welcome development for the rest of the animals. But any relief was short-lived, as the wolves all then drew large swords. This was frightening on many levels. One of them being that there were no scabbards to be seen from which to draw them; it was almost as if they had been produced out of thin air. Clearly the wolves were more threatening than they had even appeared at first.

"Corspar!!" Sarnal yelled.

From behind the wolf pack, a small iguana ran out and stood in front of him. "Right here, Your Eminence!"

He leaned down, staring into the iguana's eyes. "How does it work?"

"Well...first, they all just need to step into the square," said the iguana. "With your guards, of course. Then, give her – the fox girl – the stone from the basket she brought. She has to be the one to hold it, you see. Nobody else can hold it."

At the mention of "stone," Shadmack thought of the stones he had placed in his pockets earlier, the ones he and Joslyn had just discovered. Then he had a brilliant idea. At least, he hoped it was brilliant.

He very slowly took two of the four stones out of his pocket and quietly slipped them into Joslyn's paw. She took the stones, continuing to stare forward, but gave a quick nod of understanding to Shadmack.

"And THEN WHAT?" Sarnal shouted, continuing to interrogate the cowering lizard.

"Then, they are...transported across! Poof!" he gestured wildly with his arms. "At least that's how I understand it should happen."

The wolf glared at him for a moment, with a trace of disgust. "This had *better* work."

The iguana grinned nervously at him. "Sure," he squeaked.

"Just give her the stone."

The iguana took the stone out of the basket and handed it to the red-robed fox girl.

Shadmack noticed that the stone the iguana had handed the girl looked very similar to the ones he and Joslyn had, which gave him fresh hope.

"Now it is time for the five of you to step into the square," Sarnal growled.

"Where?" Shadmack asked.

"Right there. The square of rocks right there," he nodded in the direction of the rocks. "Step into it. Now!" said Sarnal.

"Sure, it's just that...it's not much of a square, is it?" said Shadmack.

"What do you mean?" the wolf thundered.

"Well, it's clearly slanted. Here, on the sides. I can see a parallelogram there, but it's too stretched out to be a square, really."

"He has a point, actually," said the iguana. "I mean it's definitely a quadrilateral. I'd say it's more of a *rhombus*, actually..."

"SHUT UP!" said Sarnal, swatting the reptile so that he flew several yards and smacked into one of the wolf guard's legs and sunk to the ground.

The iguana looked up at the guard. "Geometry is hard," he said, grimacing.

"It's a *Stone Square* because *I say* it's a Stone Square." He glowered at the party of five. "And *you* are stepping into *it*...now!"

Then, at sword-point, our five captive animals were led into the...Rhombus-Square. There, they were assembled into a circle,[10] backs to one another, facing outward. Shadmack turned his head slightly toward Joslyn, and they nodded.

"You should put your guards in the square alongside them also, by the way," Corspar offered as he stood and brushed off his robe.

Shadmack then pressed his extra stone into the paw of the little mouse next to him, while Joslyn did the same with the archer squirrel next to her.

Severt and Freightfurt, each standing in the circle of captives looking out at the wolf guards beyond the line of rocks, were not sure what to expect next. The last thing they expected was for the two new arrivals – a cat of some sort and a badger – standing next to them to quietly slip smooth stones into their paws. With the gags over their mouths, the only thing they could get out was questioning grunts. These quickly turned

---

[10] More of an oval, actually.

into muffled shouts of amazement when the stones they were holding, and the square they were standing in, all lit up simultaneously, flooding the clearing with light.

"NOT YET!!!" Sarnal roared, stepping forward. He rapidly motioned to his guard wolves.

"GET IN THERE! NOW!"

Sarnal's guards quickly ran forward and leapt toward the captives. But by the time they reached the square, the group of five captives had completely disappeared, and the guards ended up in a pile on top of one another as the glow of the square dimmed back to nothing.

The five Aponnans had vanished.

The Chapter with the Ruby

OUR GROUP OF ANIMAL ADVENTURERS experienced a strong feeling of falling for what felt like forever. But when it suddenly stopped, it felt like they had not been falling at all. It was as if they had just awakened from a dream of falling.

Joslyn opened her eyes and saw nothing but darkness. She blinked to be sure they were actually open. They were, and she almost poked herself painfully in the eye to prove it. She sat up and noticed she was lying on a hard surface, harder than any she had ever felt. A dark, slightly wet, hard surface. If this was Reath, it seemed like a very dank and uncomfortable place already.

She carefully slid herself across the floor until she bumped into the prone figure of another person. She could tell from the fur and quiver that it was the squirrel with the bow and arrows. He seemed to be stirring from unconsciousness as well.

"Meryam?" he asked, dazed.

"No," she said. "It's Joslyn. I'm the panther you saw back in the clearing. I don't know where the others are."

"Ah," Severt said, sitting up. He had produced a knife and freed himself from his bindings. "It is a pleasure to meet you, Lady Joslyn."

"Just Joslyn," she said.

"My name is Severt, and I am an Archer-Knight of Arrant," the squirrel continued. "I was doing routine recon near Flow territory to observe wolf movement, when we were overcome by the wolves. That's when we met you."

"Recon mission?" Joslyn asked. "I'd say you got more than you bargained for."

"Quite. I am traveling with my trusty squire, Freightfurt. He is the mouse you saw earlier."

They heard a shuffling from over to their right. "That's me," squeaked Freightfurt. "I'm over here, along with a very large rock, which is weighting me down at the moment."

"Are you hurt?" Severt called to him, concerned.

"No, just pinned down a little."

Severt crossed over to the mouse and helped Freightfurt remove the rock he was under.

"Mack?" Joslyn called, trying to locate the badger. "Are you here?"

"I'm over here," Shadmack called out. He had roused himself and made his way over to the most well-lit place in the cavern, although still very much bathed in shadow. A thin shaft of light was shining down from the ceiling above where he was standing.

"It seems I've found the exit from this cave. Or wherever this is we've been transported to."

"That's Shadmack, by the way," Joslyn said, pointing over toward the badger. "He and I work together. He's the administrator of the Aponnan Historical Society, and I help him with the...inventory, basically."

"Glad to make your acquaintance, lady and gentleman," Severt offered. "I trust we can find a source of illumination presently?"

"I think I might have found something," Shadmack said, looking up at a spot near the ceiling that was letting a little light in. Trailing down from this opening was a vine. He pulled on the vine, loosening some mud. The mud, which had been blocking a great deal of the light, fell away, letting some sunlight through.

As the room brightened, they gasped as they saw each other.

Each of the Aponnans was astounded to find that their whole appearance had changed. Instead of normal-looking Aponnan animals, the five figures standing in this room looked like *pretend* animals. It was as if they were now fake animals made of cloth, or what you or I would consider very cuddly plush toys.

"What happened to us?" said Joslyn as she held her paw up in front of her face. "Am I some kind of toy now?"

"Oh, my," Freightfurt worried. "The wolves have sentenced us to a life of being stuffed playthings! It's hopeless. What a horrid fate!"

They heard some shuffling behind them and discovered that it was Meryam, lying on the ground and trying to regain consciousness.

Severt stooped beside her with his knife, released her from her bonds, and took her hand. "M'lady, are you well?"

Her eyes fluttered open, and she started to take in the surroundings, or at least what she could, considering the still considerable lack of light.

"Just a slight headache. Otherwise I'm fine," she said, sitting up. "Where are the wolves?"

"Nowhere to be seen," said Severt. "So we can safely assume for the moment that they are still on the other side."

"Wait…" she said, looking down at her torso in shock. "What has happened to me?!"

"It's happened to all of us," Shadmack said. "There was something in the Old Scrolls about Reath that mentioned a 'change.' This must be it."

"Old Scrolls?" Severt asked.

"Yes. That's why Joslyn and I were in the Blue Mountains. To investigate some clues we had from a recent archaeological find. It appears we were onto something. Were you and the mouse and girl also searching for Reath?"

"Reath? No, not at all. I was just executing my soldier's duty of recon patrol," Severt answered. "What, pray tell, my good badger, is 'Reath'?"

"So, Mack," Joslyn interrupted, walking over to a crumpled object in the corner. "Before you start a long history lesson with our new friends, can you guys give me a hand here?"

It seemed to be a large colorful metallic bag. Joslyn had hoped her affinity for spotting precious metals would have come into play, but alas, it did not seem to be the case here. It did not *feel* anything like metal though, and when they touched it, it unfolded easily, so they could examine it more thoroughly.

Together, she, Severt, and Freightfurt tried to pull the object further into the light, but it was extremely heavy.

"Let me take a look," Severt said.

As it lay on its side, Severt stepped into the opening at its top. He was gone for a few moments, leaving the rest of the group wondering when he would emerge. When he did, he held two large orange objects, one in each hand.

"What is that? Is it food?" Freightfurt asked excitedly. He looked at the others apologetically. "Sorry. I can't recall when I had my last meal, and I am a frightfully hungry mouse."

"Before we ingest this substance," warned Shadmack, "we should examine this container from whence it came."

"Also, Sir Badger, since you seem to know of such things," Severt said to Shadmack, "there is a strange glowing object near the bottom of the bag."

Severt entered the bag again, this time with Shadmack. Those outside heard them grunting in effort, trying to carry something. A few moments later, they emerged, carrying a heavy stone. It was slightly red in color, with the letter "R" carved in the side.

"I believe we have found an actual Reathstone!" Shadmack exclaimed as he and Severt stumbled forward a few steps, under the weight of the ruby gem.

"It looks a little like the one I had back at the Clearing," Meryam noted, "but it is so much larger! I wonder if it is the same one, and if so, how did it get in the bottom of that bag?"

"At least we found yours," Joslyn said. "It looks like the four stones Mack and I brought have completely disappeared."

"Let me take a closer look," said Meryam. She walked over to Severt and Shadmack and took the stone from them, easily holding it in one hand. The Reathstone lit up much brighter when she took it.

"Interesting," Shadmack said, scratching his chin. "The Reathstone seems to activate depending on who is holding it."

"I must say, it matches your robe quite splendidly," Severt observed.

"Maybe the writing on the side of the metallic bag will offer us more clues," Shadmack said. The badger professor put on his glasses and walked over to the side of the bag to read the writing there. Meryam held up the glowing stone next to it to provide some light while he read.

"This does look a little like the Ancient Tongue, though it is written in a strange script," he said. "I'm rusty in this particular dialect, but if I am correct, it says 'Puff Cheese' or 'Cheese Puff' or something to that effect."

Freightfurt wasn't sure about the 'Puff' part. But the *'Cheese'* part was music to his little mouse ears.

"Cheese!" Freightfurt exclaimed. "Dinnertime, anyone?" he said, and he snatched one of the orange items from Severt and hefted it. "It's so light! Shall I try? Shall I?"

"Bon appétit,"[11] said Severt.

Freightfurt carefully bit into the object and took a moment to savor its flavor.

"Not cheese exactly," he said, slightly disappointed. "More air than cheese, I'm afraid. Not particularly filling either. It'll do in a pinch, but I can't see Puff Cheese being a favorite item at anyone's banquet of honor exactly."

Meryam produced a knife and, with Freightfurt's help, began slicing up the orange snacks for an impromptu dinner.

---

[11] A phrase passed down from a different Ancient Tongue.

As the group prepared to dine on Cheesy Puffs,[12] Severt suddenly stood up in front of the group to make an announcement.

"I confess," Severt announced, looking at his transformed paw, "that I am somewhat disconcerted by these recent events." Then he looked up at the others with a hint of drama. "We have found ourselves in each other's company. An unexpected surprise, but a pleasant one..." he smiled at Meryam "...to be sure."

Meryam resisted the urge to roll her eyes. Joslyn didn't resist.

"Although I wish we had met under different circumstances, my heart *still* beats within me. And it is determined to find our way home! Who is with me?"

They all half-heartedly raised their newly-stuffed paws.

"That's the spirit!" Severt said. "Now to find a way out of this pit."

He walked over to the area below where the sunlight was shining through and looked for something to climb. He grabbed the long strand of grassy vine that Shadmack had tugged on earlier and gave it a tug himself to determine how sturdy it was. The vine seemed thick enough to climb on.

"Feels pretty solid," he said. "Stay here, my friends. I shall venture forth, investigate our surroundings, and return with a full report."

---

[12] I admit, I've had less nutritious dinners myself, particularly in college.

"I'd better go with him for backup," Joslyn whispered to Shadmack. "He could probably use it." She briskly followed the exiting squirrel archer, scrambling up the vine after him.

"We'll save you some Puff Cheese!" Freightfurt called over a mouthful.

Freightfurt turned to Shadmack and Meryam. "How long do you think they will take?"

Meryam shrugged and sighed. "Your friend is brave, but he seems pretty reckless," she said to Freightfurt. "Glad the girl went with him to keep him on track."

"I have absolute faith in Joslyn," Shadmack offered. "She has a sixth sense for getting out of jams."

"I hope so," Meryam said. "You guys can sit here and wait for them if you like. I'm going to see how far back this cavern goes." She set off in the opposite direction of the fading sunlight.

"Be careful, Ma'am!" Freightfurt called after her.

While Freightfurt catnapped[13] and Meryam explored the back of the cavern, Shadmack pulled out a small piece of the parchment he had placed in his pocket with the stones when he had set out earlier that day for the Bent Tree Clearing.

---

[13] Don't tell him I called it that; it's an offensive term to mice.

In his head, he played back the scene in the Clearing with the wolves and the strange iguana... Corspar was his name. The iguana apparently knew something about Reath and the legends surrounding it as well. The iguana had been advising the Flow leader, Sarnal, but didn't seem to know that *five* stones were needed, not just one. And of course, the iguana didn't know that he and Joslyn had the other four stones.

Shadmack studied his map again. Next to the picture of the five stones, there was some scribbled handwriting that, roughly translated, said *"close set."* It was clear they would need to retrieve all five Reathstones, wherever they existed in this new world, and bring them together. But where, or how, wasn't exactly clear.

"Greetings, fellow travelers! We come to make a report!" Severt called out from the opening above them, startling Shadmack from his thoughts.

Severt slid down the vine, followed by Joslyn. "Yeah, it's definitely weird out there." Joslyn said.

"Did you see any animals?" Freightfurt asked. "Maybe we could make some friends?"

"Well, there *are* animals," Joslyn answered. "But they aren't like us. For one thing, they *don't talk,* which is pretty creepy. They just stare at you, make strange noises, and then run away. Very odd."

"Do they look like we do now? You know...stuffed?" Freightfurt asked, patting his tummy.

"No," Joslyn answered.

"Also, there are what appeared to be *thousands* of wagon-like objects as well," said Severt. "And get this – they do not require dogs or horses to propel them. And they are faster than any cart I have ever seen."

As Severt described what he had seen outside of their wet, damp cave, a growing wave of realization started to wash over Shadmack.

"Everyone," he said, "I believe I know where we are."

"Do tell, sir badger," Severt prompted.

"In the Ancient Tongue," he began, "there was a land, long described in legends, that had great riches, and many tried to seek it. But it was also full of danger... in addition to the riches."

"I believe I already know this part," Joslyn muttered.

"The wolves tried to find it," Shadmack continued, "and sent a number of their kin through the portal, but they never returned. No one knows exactly how many, but it was thought to be a very large number of wolves."

"So let me get this straight, Doc," Joslyn interjected. "Are you saying that in addition to the 'Untold Riches' and 'Change' and whatever...there is also an 'Untold' army of vicious, angry wolves lurking here somewhere?"

Shadmack nodded. "A distinct possibility."

"Great. That's really lovely," she responded.

"What is the name of this strange land, again?" Severt asked.

"Earth," Shadmack said.

"Wait," Joslyn said. "I thought you said this place was called 'Reath.' Now you're saying it's called 'Earth' instead?"

"'Reath' is the name in the *Near* Ancient tongue. But in the *Ancient* Ancient tongue? It's 'Earth.' A little confusing, I know. Don't know why it changed, really." Shadmack shrugged. "Although the modern tongues are not as keen on spelling."

"So it's called *'Earth'*?" Meryam asked. "Just *'Earth'*? as in *'dirt'*?"

"That's odd – naming your kingdom after dirt," wondered Freightfurt.

Severt nodded. "It would do us well to stay put in this cave until the morrow. Evening will approach soon. I can barely see, even here..." He suddenly stopped and looked around.

"Meryam?" He called out. "Are you here?"

"Your lady friend with the red robe?" asked Joslyn. "The one that came with you and the mouse?"

"Actually," Freightfurt corrected, "Severt and I have actually only just met her recently..."

"She was investigating to see how far back the cave went," Shadmack said. "It has been a while though."

"Alone?!" Severt said in alarm. "I must find her at once. Which way – left or right?"

Just then, a thunderous sound erupted to their left. Then it started to get louder. They all braced and turned in the direction of the sound.

"Left or right?!" Severt demanded.

"Right! Right!" Shadmack and Freightfurt called.

The four of them leapt up and scrambled down the cavern to their right.

"Meryam!" They called as the roar behind them grew to a crescendo, a cascading cacophony echoing down the corridor they were in. It was similar to the roar of the ocean, and for a good reason; it was water. *Large* quantities of it. And they could hear the liquid splashes as it flooded around corners straight for them.

The sheer magnitude of noise it was generating is hard to describe. If somebody *tried* to describe it to you, you would roll your eyes at such an exaggerated story.

If you've ever tried to outrun water, it rarely works. And it didn't work for them. The wall of gushing water crashed into them, sending them careening down the cavern maze with dizzying speed so fast that you would have slapped the ridiculous storyteller who was trying to convince you.

For the second time that day, they were carried into a dark unknown.

The Chapter with the Thread

FREIGHTFURT CLUNG DESPERATELY TO A PIECE of debris. It was buoyant and was barely larger than the mouse, and he was able to use it as a raft for the current. If he were on holiday, this would have been a fairly enjoyable amusement ride, except for not knowing how it ended, and also that he could not see anything in the darkness. And he was afraid of being separated from the others. So, actually, it was nothing like an enjoyable ride. Quite the opposite. I don't know why I said that.

Thankfully, the darkness aspect was about to be remedied though, as he peered ahead and saw an opening with sunlight growing closer. He swiftly reached it, the wall of water propelling him into the outdoors, where he landed in a river. The river had a gentle current, and he was able to paddle with his furry paws over to the bank, where he had a little lie down and tried to calm his shattered nerves.

"Freightfurt!" he heard Severt call suddenly. "Are you hurt?" he asked for the second time that day.

"I don't think so," he said. "But I've been better."

"Same goes for all of us," Shadmack agreed, walking over to join them and wringing out his tunic. "I don't like the look of this place at all."

Severt helped Freightfurt stand to his feet, and together, the three of them were astonished at what they saw.

All around them, near the bank of the river they had just climbed out of and beyond, were many exceedingly tall, boxy structures, much like the schoolhouses and granaries of their home. Everywhere, bright surfaces reflected sunlight in all directions. Frightening noises emanated from all directions. To the eyes and ears of our animal friends, it was complete chaos.

Large metal objects, or creatures of some sort, sped back and forth on a hard path nearby. Shadmack and Freightfurt recognized these as the wagons that Severt had described earlier. They were very noisy, and smoke emitted behind them as they moved.

They didn't see any animals – talking or otherwise – except for the occasional bug. And those didn't seem too chatty.

"I am so sorry I ate whatever it is that gave me such a dream," Freightfurt regretted. "*Terribly* sorry. Curse that Puff Cheese!"

"If I were to guess," Shadmack guessed, "I would say that we just came out of some sort of drainage system. Or, perhaps, irrigation of some kind."

"Whatever it was, I, for one, am glad it is behind us now," Severt said, shaking water out of his hat. "Our next course of action should likely be to find our lady companions. It looks as if the water forced them to a different exit than ours. If we walk further along this bank, maybe we can find another opening."

Severt climbed on top of a small tree trunk. "Let me see – the position of the sun in the sky is there." He pointed.

"If we walk eastward, perhaps we will have more daylight," Shadmack offered.

"Yes, and it also seems to be the direction of slope for the stream...in which to..." He trailed off suddenly as he stared at the sky.

"Yes?" Shadmack asked. "In which to what?"

"Do you see it?" Severt asked, squinting into the air.

"What? The sun?" said Shadmack. "It's rather hard to miss."

"Not the sun – that line in the sky, just so." Severt picked up a stick and pointed.

"Where?"

"Right there, several feet up."

"You must be going loopy in this strange world," said Shadmack. "I see no line in the sky."

Freightfurt turned his head a little, and a look of understanding came across his face. He twitched his whiskers.

"Indeed, I do see *something*," the mouse said. "It's very faint, but definitely something there."

"I don't know what you two are going on about. *What* lines? Are you mad?" asked Shadmack. 'Invisible lines,'" he harrumphed.

"Not invisible, just transparent... Freightfurt, if you can see it, can you come over here? I'd really like to try to reach it... Or at least have *you* do so."

Freightfurt walked over and crawled up on Severt's shoulders. He extended his arm as much as he could stretch. "Nope, I can't reach it," He said, straining as high as he could.

Shadmack sighed. "Are we quite done yet? I would like to get out of this noise."

Severt looked over and saw a patch of grass that was elevated higher than the tree trunk he had been standing on before. He walked over to the knoll and climbed it to get closer and see if he could lay a finger on the puzzling object.

It was like a gossamer thread stretching as far as he could see in opposite directions. He stretched out his hand but it remained just out of reach, even when he used the stick. No matter what he stood on, it was still just a mite away from his grasp.

He was reminded of his childhood days when he would see a rainbow so clear and crisp; he could imagine crashing through it if he could just get close enough.

On more than one of these occasions, he would grab the nearest horse-friend he could find and ride toward the rainbow. He would ride and ride until the horse would not put up with him anymore and eventually would dump him aside and head back to the village. But no matter how far he rode, he couldn't reach the rainbow. It would remain on the horizon, like rainbows always do, until they fade away or are just forgotten as your attention turns to something else.

This line in the sky was like that – much nearer, but no less difficult to touch.

Severt decided that he would walk a ways under it to see what it was connected to. But as soon as he took a step down in the opposite direction, it disappeared.

"Where did it go?" he said. "It appears to have gone away!"

"Yet I still see it," Freightfurt said.

"Come over here," Severt said. Freightfurt walked over to him, tracing his footsteps underneath the line. The mouse frowned as he looked up and also discovered it had vanished as soon as he walked in the opposite direction.

"I have lost sight of it as well, I'm afraid," he said, disappointed.

"What a pity," said Shadmack, growing impatient. "Can we move along, then? Presumably, after a drink of water you will feel better and not experience such delusions."

But Severt and Freightfurt had already returned to their original spot and discovered that they could now see the line again! This time they walked along underneath it, but going in the opposite direction from the one they had done previously. And this time, it did *not* disappear as they walked beneath it.

"Ah!" gathered Severt. "If we walk in one direction, it *disappears*. But if we walk in the other direction, it *remains*. I suppose we are meant to follow it in a specific direction *so that it stays in view*."

To test this theory, he took a step backwards, and the thread left his view. Then he took a step forward in repair, and it reappeared. "Yes, indeed," he concluded.

"What about Joslyn?" Shadmack said, worried about his lost companion. "And...Meryam?" This last was obviously meant to pique the squirrel's interest.

"The sky-line is leading us in an eastward direction anyway," said Severt. "Perhaps it will lead us to her... er, them."

"Well, I suppose if no one has a better idea, we can just follow your...thread, then." Shadmack conceded.

The badger sighed and followed Severt, Freightfurt, and their messenger in the sky that he could not see.

The Chapter with Mott

J OSLYN LEAPT FURIOUSLY FROM ONE PIECE OF debris to another as they raced down the dark tunnel, propelled by the rush of water. Her panther reflexes carried her from one to the other fairly easily, but it was still difficult to do in the very faint light. She was glad to see that the light showing at the end of the tunnel was getting brighter and larger. Then she was immediately less glad when she considered that she did not know what was on the other side of it.

She found out soon enough, as the opening quickly overtook her and she was thrust out of it, flying through the air and landing in some tall grass. The water from the pipe she had just exited splashed down all around her and flowed off to a stream on her right.

Joslyn took a deep breath, grateful to have had a soft place to land. She checked to see if she had all of her belongings. It seemed that she still had everything. She then checked to see if she could see any of the others;

she couldn't. Apparently they had been flushed out of a different exit.

So Joslyn was alone. Not a terrible thing; Joslyn had always worked better alone anyway. Supposedly she was now in a land full of adventure and Untold Riches. She was a big fan of both of those things.

She hoped the others were okay, particularly Shadmack. But for now, she had better turn her attention to getting out of the area she was now trapped in.

Joslyn was completely surrounded by a tall fence. The fence was very solid, and she could see no opening. She also noticed that there was what appeared to be a string, or spider web or something, stretching from one side of the enclosure to the other.

She walked over to get a closer look at the fence, to survey the materials it was made of and investigate any weak points it might have structurally. She also hoped to find out what that weird string was.

But as she neared the fence, the ground suddenly gave way beneath her.

She fell several feet down and ungracefully landed in a large pile of dirt. It was a large enough fall to hurt, but not to *get* hurt, thankfully.

She started to stand up and then quickly startled and sat down again as a giant face thrust itself at her. She backed up to get a better view and discovered that the face belonged to a rather large groundhog.

"Whoa! Stand back!" She exclaimed, drawing her knife. "Who are you?"

The groundhog stared at her a moment, not appearing to comprehend her question.

Then she remembered her previous brief foray with Severt, where they had discovered that the animals in this world didn't seem to have the capacity to talk.

The groundhog then simply chittered at her and ran away, disappearing through a tunnel. The tunnel looked like it had been recently dug by some animal. It occurred to her that it had probably been dug by the groundhog she had just met. Joslyn was somewhat envious of animals with claws that could dig tunnels so efficiently. There were so many good uses for tunneling. You could do it to hide, sneak up on people... and to get under fences.

The groundhog may not have been an engaging conversationalist. But he *was* a genius in his own way.

Emerging from the tunnel on the other side of the fence, she found herself in a ditch with a steady flow of water running down it. On either side were steep walls of dirt. Joslyn had had her fill of water so far on this adventure, but at least this stream was of a relatively slower current compared to the life-threatening kind she had encountered earlier.

Should she start hopping from rock to rock to get downstream?

She traced the sides of the ditch walls with her eyes to see if there was any purchase to be found for her feet – some way that she would be able to climb up one side or the other. There did not seem to be anything but smooth dirt. The walls of the ditch were too close on either side of the stream, leaving no river bank of any kind to walk along it, so hopping on the rocks seemed to be the only option.

But as she scanned higher on the dirt wall, she was surprised to see the string in the air again, the same one she had spotted earlier in the previous fenced-in area. It was running as far as she could see downstream, hovering in the air above it.

Perhaps if she could find where it connected behind her, she could fashion some sort of zip line. She had always been a champion zip liner, and she had a few items in her bag that might help her do the trick.

The line was pretty high up there though, so she would have to walk back to find a place to reach it. But whenever she tried to turn away from it, the darn thing would disappear.

She tried several different angles, but it was hopeless. Every time she made a move that wasn't downstream, the string would vanish from view.

So much for the zip lining idea, she thought.

"Hullo," said a voice suddenly from her left.

Joslyn whipped around and pulled out her knife. It was immediately pulled from her hand.

"Ow. That's sharp!" The voice yelped. Joslyn looked around wildly, trying to spot the voice bouncing off the canyon walls. "Just kidding. Didn't really touch it. Would've hurt if I did though."

Joslyn was about as confused as you about now. She kept turning in circles to find who was making these strange comments while disarming her.

"Show yourself!" she yelled.

"Or you'll do what?"

"I'll…I'll think of something!"

"No! Don't do that! Don't '*think of something*'!" the voice exclaimed in mock terror. "Please! Anything but thinking of something! Have mercy!"

A monkey-like figure jumped into view on the rock opposite her, holding her knife.

He had covered his face with large fingers. Then he separated them, peering out. "I kid again. That's not scary at all."

He harmlessly tossed the knife over toward Joslyn, and it stuck in the rock near her feet.

"What are you?" Joslyn asked incredulously. "Some kind of monkey?"

"No! I am *not* a monkey," he said, slightly offended. "I am a *sloth*."

"Common mistake though," he continued. "Many people think sloths are monkeys, when actually, the two are not the same at all. Sloths are more like anteaters, or armadillos." He cupped his hands around his mouth. "Hulloooo! Education up in here!"

"You move pretty fast for a sloth," Joslyn said.

"Correct! I am a *fast sloth*. Not slow, like other sloths. You could call me a 'Foth,' I guess." He hopped over to the rock she was standing on. "I was picked on a lot in school for not being as slow as all the other sloths. Very hurtful."

"I don't have time for this," Joslyn said, bewildered, pulling the knife from the stone and hopping to the next one.

"That's what *I* said! Bullies will be bullies, though. Where are you going?"

"I'm following…something."

The sloth flashed by her suddenly and stopped in her path of progress, again.

"A *thread*?" He frantically examined the air around them. "You see a thread, don't you! Where is it? Where is it?" he asked, hopping up and down excitedly.

"Right above your head." She gestured in the direction.

"Above *my* head? Well, then…perhaps *I am your destiny*." He hopped over to a rock two feet to his left and looked up. "Did it move?"

"No."

"Whew," he sighed, looking coyly at the ground. "That would've been awkward."

"So where did you come from, exactly?" she asked.

"Over there," he said, pointing at the original spot he had first said "Hullo" to her.

"No, I mean, are you also from Aponna?"

"A what?"

"Aponna. It's the world I came from. Animals talk there too. So I thought possibly you might be from there also."

"Oh, Aponna!" he said in recognition. Then frowned. "Never heard of it," he said. "Except for a little bit. Actually, I think I grew up there-*ish*." He paused. "Yes, I think I might be from Aponna."

The sloth's double talk was beginning to wear on Joslyn's nerves. "So how did you get to Earth then?" she asked.

"Earth? No, no – you see, it's pronounced '*Reath*.'"

"'Earth,' 'Reath,' whatever," Joslyn said, frustrated. "How did *you* get *here*?"

"A stone brought me," he said. "I think."

Joslyn froze. "What stone?" she asked earnestly.

He pointed downstream, in the direction of both the river's current and the thread she could still see glowing brightly in the air. "Somewhere over in that direction. You'll need it if you want to get back to where you came from."

"My name's Mott, by the way." He pulled out a brightly colored stick from the bag slung over his shoulder and offered it to her. "Would you like a lollipop? I have two."

"Joslyn. And, er, no thanks," she said, waving off the lollipop. "So there's a stone *that* way..."

Since the current, the thread, and the sloth wanted her to go downstream, she decided she might as well not resist any longer and head that direction.

"Let's go," she said.

The sloth rock-hopped behind her, enjoying his lollipop.

The Chapter with the Emerald

AFTER A FEW HOURS' JOURNEY, THE OTHER HALF of the company, composed of Severt, Freightfurt, and Shadmack, arrived at a building of some sort. The thread that Severt and Freightfurt could still see extended to the door on the front, and as such, they concluded that they should enter. But of course, the door was fairly large; the door latch was high and out of reach for them and was unlikely to be unlocked in any case.

They looked around the base of the building and could not find any other point of entry. Suddenly, they heard a loud slam and what sounded like loud retreating footsteps. Deciding to investigate, they turned the corner on the building and discovered another smaller door. This one was cracked open. They opened it large enough for them to squeeze through and went inside.

The inside of the house, if indeed it *was* a house – was full of large furniture that would only be suitable for giants in the eyes of our Aponnan friends. Strange objects and small structures lay all around that seemed to indicate that this was indeed a house where giants lived. Their eyes drank in each of these new sights in turn as they made their way toward the location of the front of the house to see if Severt or Freightfurt could regain sight of their thread that had been cut off at the door on the other side.

Eventually, they found themselves in the foyer. Severt and Freightfurt were glad to see the thread in the air again. It was there extending from the front door toward the foot of some stairs that led to the upper story of the building.

"I believe we are meant to ascend," Severt announced to the group. The other two nodded, and the three approached the stairs to climb them.

There were seventeen in all, and when they reached the landing, they stopped for a minute to catch their breath. Severt was less out of breath than the other two, of course, but it had been quite an ascent for even a stout soldier.

They were now in a corridor with tall walls and a high ceiling. Various doorways could be seen in the hallway.

"Let us see what lies in this abode…" Severt started, when all of a sudden, they heard a loud noise that sounded as if a large bear were spouting gibberish.[14]

---

[14] By a strange coincidence, bears in Aponna are actually known for spouting gibberish. Many think that early in their ancestry, young bears often tried to conduct conversations while having mouths stuffed full of honey. This resulted in unintelligible grunts and such, and soon they would often speak this way all the time, to the consternation of other non-bear animals that were around them who could not understand a word they were saying. Eventually, bear parents became more successful at teaching their kids to enunciate. Along with enforcing the principle that good bear cubs shouldn't talk with their mouths full.

"What manner of creature can that be?" Severt exclaimed, and they took a few steps backward.

The sound had come from one of the doorways ahead and to the left. They cautiously made their way in that direction.

When they peered around the corner, they did not see any type of monstrous beast that could have made such a horrible noise.

What they *did* see was a small stuffed raccoon, sitting about four feet away from them in a small chair at a desk. There were streaks of gray shooting through much of his black fur, which, mixed with the white, gave the appearance of an elderly animal. The desk was just one in a large assortment of desks, all facing a much *larger* desk with a chalkboard situated behind it. Several books were arranged on this large desk, as if a teacher should have been there doing teacher-y things.

"It appears to be a school of some sort," Shadmack whispered. "Fascinating."

"Be careful, Mr. Professor," Severt warned. "We haven't yet determined the source of that loud bear-like noise. I expect a large beast in this place – *more* than one even–lurking about. Perhaps you and Freightfurt should take shelter while I investigate." Severt indicated a shelf-like structure near the wall of the corridor.

"Right-o!" said Freightfurt and scrambled under the shelf.

Shadmack had started to turn to join him, when suddenly he saw the raccoon at the desk winking at him.

"Did you see that?" he asked Severt. "He just winked at us!"

"I did not witness that," Severt said, "though I trust you to be a man of integrity who would not lie. I do not trust *him* as much though. I wonder what his game is. If he is *winking* at us..."

They looked at the raccoon together, and Severt gave him a slight wave. The raccoon winked at them again.

"Maybe he is just being friendly," Freightfurt offered in a whisper from his position beneath the shelf.

"Perhaps he needs help," said Severt. "And he is signaling us for rescue." He thought a moment. "Or else, he could be laying a trap..."

They were about to move a little closer to speak to the stoic, winking raccoon – and question him about the large giant bear-like sound they had heard earlier – when suddenly a hand grabbed the raccoon. A *very large* hand – like a gorilla's, but very smooth – grabbed the raccoon and the chair, picked them both up, turned them completely around backwards, and then set them down again. Now, the raccoon was facing the wall, instead of away from it. The owner of the large hand emitted more gibberish.

"What was that? Is he still winking?" Freightfurt asked in a valiant effort to continue to be a part of the conversation while remaining safely under the shelf.

Severt decided to not tell the easily frightened mouse about the large hand just yet.

Just then, Shadmack picked a strange time to be brave. You see, his instinct for avoiding danger was only trumped by his penchant for discovering new knowledge. When a person who is in love with academics as much as Shadmack was discovers not just a new world, but a *classroom* in a strange, new world... well, that is just too much to resist, large bellowing beasts or not.

Before Severt could stop him, Shadmack had already crept through the doorway and half-way to where the raccoon was. Now that he could see the whole room, he noticed that in addition to the classroom area where the raccoon was sitting there was also a bed, what looked like a large strange-looking lantern, a large mirror, a chest with drawers, and a lot of what looked like children's toys. Apparently he was inside the bedroom of some kind of giant child.

Then, when Shadmack had almost reached the raccoon, he looked up and saw the hairless, non-bear giant.

When Shadmack was a young badger, his best friend was a possum named Shrelvurt. Now possums, as you know, are very good at playing dead. And Shrelvurt was the best. In fact, he competed quite often in the sport, winning varsity competitions throughout most of his years of upper school. He was that good. He could play dead anywhere and anytime, and there were many obituaries written that had to be revoked in the wake of his formidable talents. Eventually, Shrelvurt's celebrity eclipsed his skills; no one believed him anymore, and he had to retire from the practice.

But during their time growing up together, Shadmack had learned a few good tips from Shrelvurt on how best to play dead. Techniques such as how to look as if taking your last breath, sudden lack of forward progress, staggering, asking if anyone else is seeing the angels, etc. But sometimes, just a good high quality fall-down would do the trick.

So, even though badgers are not typically as skilled as possums at playing dead, a badger that was *best friends* with a champion dead-faker could do a pretty good job.

Thanks, Shrelvurt, Shadmack thought and flopped over.

From their hallway perspective, Severt and Freightfurt could not see what Shadmack had seen, but from Shadmack's reaction, they assumed it was the creature that the smooth-skinned hand belonged to.

"Alas!" Severt whispered loudly, still not able to see the giant beast. "The poor badger! That creature must be frightening to behold!!"

Then the same hairless hand grasped Shadmack and lifted *him* up and out of sight. Severt pulled a bow from his quiver and mentally weighed if this situation could now be considered a fray, and whether he should enter into it.

Before he could take a step, the giant hairless hand placed Shadmack, now recovering from his phony swoon, in a chair next to the raccoon, who was also still facing the wall.

Shadmack had hoped to examine the room and his surroundings further but was discouraged that all he could see now was the wall he was facing, unless he turned around or looked over his shoulder, which would be hard to do without attracting the attention of the giant again.

He had gathered that playing dead, or perhaps just staying still, would keep the giant creature at bay. And from what he could tell from observing the raccoon, this did seem to be the best strategy.

Quick, sideways glances confirmed that there were many other cloth animals in the large classroom area, sitting at desks and tables. But only he and the raccoon were facing the wall.

"I wonder why we should be the only ones facing backwards against this wall," Shadmack whispered aloud to himself.

"Because you and I are in *'Time Out,'*" the raccoon whispered back, startling Shadmack, almost into real unconsciousness, rather than the fake kind he had done earlier.

"You speak!" Shadmack exclaimed in a whisper. "You actually know *words*?"

"Yes. And apparently I use them too much," said the raccoon. "I am currently in Time Out as a punishment because I was 'talking too much' during class."

The raccoon leaned toward Shadmack slightly, smiling. "And get this – *so did you*."

"What?! That's preposterous. I have only just arrived," said Shadmack, "and I would never visit with other students during class. It's improper."

He looked over toward the doorway. Freightfurt had finally gathered the nerve to come out from under the shelf and join Severt at the doorway, where they were both now sticking their heads around the corner to observe Shadmack and the raccoon. Shadmack gave a slight wave, and they waved back.

"Since you speak," he addressed the raccoon, "could you tell me…what is this place? And what type of creature *is* that, making all of us sit here, punishing us under false pretenses?"

"She is a creature called a 'human,'" the raccoon explained. "A human child named Sally. And she is *playing* school with us and the other animals – er, toy animals, actually. She thinks we are toy animals as well, you see."

"Speaking of 'playing,'" the raccoon continued, "that was a great job you did playing dead earlier. And just in the nick of time; she almost saw you moving."

"This 'Sally' seems a fearsome creature," Shadmack said. Then he reconsidered a moment. "But if she advocates learning in a classroom environment, she can't be all bad, I suppose."

"She's adopted me as a favorite 'toy' and, over time, has become somewhat of a friend," the raccoon said. "It doesn't seem that long ago when I also came here from your world, many moons ago."

"My stars!" exclaimed Shadmack. "So the legends *are* true."

"Some of them," said the Raccoon.

"I have read many books about this place," said Shadmack. "But so far, they have not helped me understand Reath – or Earth, rather – very much at all."

"Perhaps you are just reading the wrong ones," the Raccoon said and cracked opened the book on the desk in front of him. Shadmack leaned over to see what was written there.

But instead of seeing pages inside, the book had been completely hollowed out, and in the center of it sat a glowing emerald Reathstone with the letter "E" carved in the side.

"The name's Stryton," the raccoon said, extending a paw. "Pleasure to make your acquaintance."

As the raccoon and Shadmack were having this discussion, Severt and Freightfurt were still observing them a few yards away from the doorway.

"Clearly, if we are to rescue Shadmack, we must dispatch the monstrous foe that holds them captive," Severt said.

"Um, Severt, look at that toy Raccoon. I think he is *speaking* to Shadmack," Freightfurt observed. "And they do not seem as frightened as they were before."

"Indeed. Let us join in their discussion," Severt said as he quietly led Freightfurt into the room.

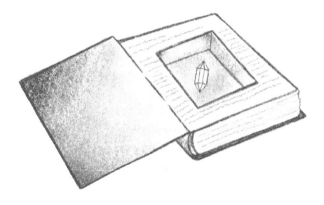

"I am sorry to interrupt," Severt urged Shadmack and the raccoon as he approached, "but I think we should find higher ground before that monster returns!"

"She is no monster," the elderly raccoon responded. "She is named Sally and – based on how long she has been away now – she is probably having dinner with her mother at the moment. She won't be back for a while."

Severt leaned in close and looked in the raccoon's eyes.

"Perhaps you are in league with the Sally," he said.

"In what?"

"In league. With it. The monster. The Sally."

Shadmack waved him off.

"Severt, I'd like you to meet Stryton. He is a fellow sojourner from Aponna – Tumblestock village, to be precise. And he carries a Reathstone," Shadmack said, pointing at the raccoon's glowing book. "He is friends with the giant. He says she is a child – a creature called a 'human.'"

Severt paused. This was a lot to take in.

"Sally is practically family," Stryton said. "I have lived here a while now with both her and her mother."

"And does she also have a father?" asked Severt, trying to get a grasp of how many giants might be around.

"Yes, but he left the picture shortly after I arrived. I don't know why. He was just here one day, gone the next. I have not seen him for a long time now," Stryton explained. "So it is just the girl and her mother."

Stryton looked over toward the door. "It looks like your friend has found a thread," he gestured at Freightfurt, who was still over by the door.

Freightfurt was pointing up at the ceiling and whispering the words "A Thread!" excitedly to them.

"Can *you* see a thread?" Severt asked Stryton.

"No," Stryton sighed. "I have not seen *any* threads actually. Not since I ended up here, in Sally's room."

"Why is that?"

"I don't know. Perhaps because I didn't think I needed them. Or maybe because I am already where I am supposed to be. But clearly you – or at least your mouse friend – are still seeing them and need to continue your journey. I would advise you to follow them while you can. I will come with you to assist getting through the house. But I should warn you: Sally also has a pet dog. His name is Perky, and he is a delight." He said this last sentence with a tinge of sarcasm.

They made their way toward the door and back out into the hallway.

The Chapter with the Choice

JOSLYN AND HER NEW SLOTH COMPANION HAD been hopping from rock to rock for a while. Rock hopping was not a favorite of Joslyn's, but apparently it *was* a favorite of the sloth's.

"Ooo, there's a good one over there...six feet away, maybe? Can you hold this?" He held out his lollipop. She refused to take it.

The sloth's chattering was annoying, and Joslyn was beginning to hope he would go jump off a cliff.

Coincidentally, a cliff was now coming into view as Joslyn neared the end of the stream amidst the sound of rushing water. There was a waterfall up ahead!

As long as she stayed on the rocks, and out of the water, she felt she would be safe.

When she finally arrived at the waterfall and looked down, she saw there were two other lower cliffs, with the waterfall dropping between them to the very distant ground beyond.

One of the cliffs had the largest piece of gold Joslyn had ever seen. Just by the size of it, she knew it would fetch thousands of leafs back in Aponna. Joslyn would be a very rich cat. Untoldly Rich. This world was *finally delivering*!

However, on the other cliff, she saw Meryam, the red-robed girl she had met earlier in their journey through the portal. She was lying still – unmoving, but apparently uninjured.

Red Robe seems to have gotten herself in trouble again, she thought.

The glistening gold nugget beckoned gloriously. But could she, in good conscience, ignore a fellow traveler-in-need in order to snag treasure? Joslyn admitted she held some resentment toward Meryam. The main reason they were all in this mess was because the fox had been too cozy with the Flow to begin with. Perhaps Meryam deserved to tough it out alone in this place after all.

And the beautiful gold lying there? It was the first 'Untold Riches'-like thing she had yet seen in this place.

"Dilemma time: Gold? Or the girl?" the annoying sloth said, peering over the edge with her. "What does your thread say?"

Joslyn had completely forgotten about the thread. One of the strangest things about the thread was when she first saw it, it was all she could think about. But as soon as she started hopping over the rocks, she forgot all about it. It's pretty strange to have a guide in the sky telling you which way to go, but stranger still to so easily forget it's even there.

She looked up and noticed that the thread *was* still there, but it had done a hard ninety-degree turn downward, directly toward the rock cliff that the girl was lying on. If the thread was telling the truth, then going to the fox girl should be her next objective.

Joslyn sighed. Perhaps she could find a way to circle back to the gold later on, if nobody else nabbed it by then.

She looked through her pack and found some stakes, some rope, and a harness. Just what she needed for rappelling down to Meryam's rock outcropping.

She found three large rocks that seemed to be very sturdy and firmly planted in the riverbed, arranged in a triangle. She staked all three of them, threaded the rope through, and attached her harness. Then she started to gently lower herself. The sloth waved from the rocks above and offered her wishes of luck, and also offered a couple of lollipops for her and Meryam. She accepted the first offer but declined the second.

After a few minutes of lowering herself, she reached the rock surface next to Meryam. She examined her and found her to be unconscious but breathing well. Her hair and clothing were soaked through, indicating she had endured a rough ride down the stream and over the falls. The fox was very fortunate that she had landed where she did, instead of being taken even further down the waterfall. But it was *unfortunate,* Joslyn thought, that she hadn't also landed where there was a large hunk of gold.

Joslyn jostled the unconscious Meryam but couldn't get her to wake. It was going to be difficult to carry her, especially since there didn't seem to be any stepping stones down the falls.

That's when she remembered her earlier zip lining idea. With the rope from her pack, she quickly set to work putting it into action.

A while later, Joslyn slid to a halt in her makeshift sling and untied the lasso from the branch of a tree. The rope in her bag had been just long enough for her to wrestle up a zip line from the cliff she had found Meryam and the nearest tree. Thankfully, it had held the weight of the two of them as they slid down the line from her previous spot to the ground below.

She set Meryam's still-unconscious form on the ground and examined her face. It seemed to be the face of a girl who was very pampered and had probably never worked a day in her life.

Spoiled brat, probably, she thought.

Joslyn was almost finished packing the equipment bag into her bag, when she heard Meryam stirring.

"Where am I?" she asked groggily.

"Safe on dry ground," Joslyn said. "You were washed onto a cliff. I saw you there and zip lined you down. You're welcome."

"Oh. Um, thanks then," Meryam said, rubbing her eyes.

As her head cleared, Meryam remembered the Reathstone in her pack and opened it to observe its softly glowing lustre. "I wonder where the other four Reathstones are."

"You and me both, Red," Joslyn said.

"We'll need them all, apparently," Meryam said, "if we are to get back home to Aponna."

Joslyn looked up longingly at the overhang where the large cache of gold lay out of sight from their vantage point below.

"Perhaps there is a market of some type nearby where we can find some gear. There's something up there I'd like to check out later."

"You want to go back up there?" Meryam asked, puzzled.

Joslyn spotted one of the squarish buildings on the horizon. "I think I see something ahead. Let's head over that way."

Meryam nodded and followed behind her.

"And if you happen to see anything weird in the sky," Joslyn said, "like a thread or anything like that, let me know right away."

The Chapter with the Squearl

BACK IN THE WORLD OF APONNA, SARNAL tapped his claws impatiently. He was always annoyed when his servants were late. Such was the case again with Corspar, the iguana historian that was advising him over this whole affair. Sarnal was not much for taking advice, nor for tardiness in those who were supposed to be supplying it.

The door to Sarnal's room flew open, and in sped Corspar with his tail twitching behind him.

"Sorry, Your Greatness!" he exclaimed. "I was held up by the weather; it was so lovely I had to pause and admire it." He laughed nervously. Sarnal did not laugh. "Just kidding...it was actually bad weather..."

Sarnal despised the reptile. He also hated depending on creatures that were not wolves to make his plans. But Corspar's talents were unique, and he had proved himself loyal thus far.

Corspar produced a large square-ish object that seemed to be made of translucent pearl. "I have news," he said. "*Good* news, based on the readings from the Squearl."

"What squirrel?" Sarnal asked. "There are no squirrels in my employ!" He hated the notion of consorting with rodents even more than consorting with reptiles.

"Actually *this* Squearl," he held up the pearl object. "It's a square pearl – hence, 'Squearl.' You see?"

Sarnal grunted.

"I don't know how people think it's a square though," the lizard wondered aloud. "It's actually more like..."

"If you tell me it's a rhombus," Sarnal snarled, "I will kill you where you stand."

The iguana gulped. "It's a Squearl," he whispered.

"Get on with it. What news?"

"It has changed color," Corspar said. "Which would indicate that the Flow on the Other Side are now in close proximity to the Aponnans that went through earlier."

Sarnal leaned forward and examined the square pearl. "So this 'Squearl' is essentially like a transmitter that keeps us abreast of what is happening on the Other Side?"

"Yes!" Corspar answered. "For those who know how to use it," he hastily added. It was important, for his sake, to impress on Sarnal his continued usefulness.

"What colors do we want to see," he asked, "O Keeper of the Squearl?" This last was ironic respect.

"Yellow is good," Corspar said. "Orange is better." He leaned in. "But Red is the best."

"If the Aponnans find the stones, then that would be 'better'?" Sarnal asked.

"Yes," Corspar nodded. "Orange!"

"And if our Flow are with the the Aponnans *and* the stones?"

"Red, Your Preeminence," Corspar said.

Sarnal smiled.

The Chapter with the Turquoise

"So, Stryton, tell me again about the threads," Shadmack said to the wizened raccoon. "Why should we follow them?"

"Because the threads show you where you should go," said Stryton. "They tend to show up when you are least expecting it; but then sometimes they *don't* show up when you would like them to. And they sometimes lead you in directions you don't want to go, even when you feel like you should follow them anyway."

"I see."

Shadmack looked up toward the ceiling as if addressing one. "Hey, Thread! Can you show us where to go next?"

"It doesn't work like that, I'm afraid," said Stryton.

"Who hung these threads?" asked Shadmack.

"I don't know. Apparently it was done a long time ago by whoever made the Reathstones, but that is just conjecture." He pointed just off to the left as they descended the last step. "Speaking of Reathstones..."

There, in the corner, was what looked like a large turquoise stone with a chain and a clasp attached! Carved in the side of the stone was the letter "T."

"It looks like a giant earring," said Stryton, "like something Sally would wear, if she were older. In fact, I believe I do remember Sally wearing it as an earring," Stryton added, "but she has long forgotten it, I believe."

"Is it heavy?" asked Severt.

"Yes...heavier than it should be," said Stryton.

Severt walked over and picked it up.

"It does not appear to be heavy," Severt said, hefting it easily.

"Yes, if the Reathstones are keyed to a specific person, they will glow and be easily lifted by that person."

Severt remembered this occurring with Meryam when she had picked up the stone they found in the Puff Cheese bag.

He then marveled again at what cruel fate had thrust him and the beautiful fox girl apart just as he was beginning to gain her acquaintance.

"Well, if this is an earring, they usually come in pairs," Shadmack observed. "So perhaps there is another Reathstone around here to go with it. Tell me, Stryton, have you seen another one like it around?"

"Yes. But acquiring it will likely *not* be easy. The last I saw, it was located in the..."

Stryton was cut off by another voice, very low, very gruff, and very unfriendly.

It said: "The basement."

They turned to look for the source of the voice and were horrified to find it. Severt quickly notched an arrow and took aim, with Freightfurt quickly jumping behind him, shaking.

Do you, dear reader, remember how our adventurers had taken on a new form in this new world[15]? They now looked like stuffed animal toys. And what they saw in front of them now was a very disagreeable stuffed toy wolf.

While the new forms of our adventuring party from Aponna were very pleasant and similar to something that you would gladly snuggle with at night to go to sleep, the wolf they now looked upon was not. While he was a little less terrifying to behold than a large Flow wolf would have been in Aponna, he was still a terrifying sight.

On the wolf's face, there were plastic buttons where the eyes would have been...but only one, you see, because the other had been pulled out and some of the stuffing from inside his head was protruding from the spot. Some of the thread that had held it in place

---

[15] A new world to them, but an old one to us, of course.

was trailing down the side of his face, like whiskers that had been misplaced. The fur on the top of his head wore smudges throughout, as if he had been thrown in mud weeks ago, never cleaned, and now was permanently stained. The seam that ran down his back was threadbare, and some stuffing was poking out at intervals here and there, and the same could be said of the joint where his front left leg met his body.

In short, he looked like a very mistreated toy. Clearly, as a wolf, his intentions were less than kindly, and the disconcerting nature of his appearance did not help him in the charisma department.

"I *thought* there was a Reathstone in the basement," Stryton muttered. "Of course, it *would* be guarded by Gronnal." He indicated the ugly wolf in front of them.

"Where is the Reathstone, wolf?" Severt demanded. "Speak out! I doubt you have the character to lift it. Perhaps I can give it a try."

"Tell me," the wolf sneered. "How is my brother doing? It's been *so* long since I have seen him."

"Are you talking about Sarnal?" Shadmack asked. "He's your brother?"

"Yes, indeed. My *dear* brother; he and I are very close." Gronnal took a few steps toward them. "And *you* are going to help reunite us."

Suddenly, a loud growling sound filled the hallway. Then there came the even louder sound of a dog barking.

"Tell that to Perky," said Stryton, smiling. They could hear the paws of Sally's pet dog scrambling across the floor in a nearby room.

The wolf looked down the hallway with a look of concern. He then turned away and strode a few steps toward a vent in the floor. "This isn't over," he said. "There's only one way home... And it's *through us*." He leapt through the vent, and it closed behind him.

The band of Aponnans turned to Stryton, obviously wanting to know who Perky was.

"How can this Perky be any safer than the wolf?" asked Freightfurt, still huddled behind Severt. "Sounds like he's just another frightening beast!"

"It's Sally's dog," said Stryton. "He does like to...'play'...with stuffed animals. But never fear – I can stall Perky. But I'm afraid we'll need to get you out of the house."

He led them down the last few stairs and across the foyer.

The Chapter with the Yard

THE FENCE WAS MADE OF METAL, OR AT LEAST that's what it looked like to Joslyn. A web of metal with interlocking strands. There were plenty of diamond-shaped holes in the fence, but unfortunately, they were all too small for Joslyn and Meryam to squeeze through.

"So, you still don't see any threads?" Joslyn asked Meryam. She had described the thread that she had seen earlier to Meryam. Joslyn had lost sight of hers, and she was hoping that Meryam might be able to see something. But Joslyn wasn't too optimistic about this; Meryam didn't appear to be the most perceptive person, or to make good judgments. And there were still too many unanswered questions around the fox girl.

"So, I have a question," Joslyn said.

"Me too. Just what kind of creature lives in a place like this?" Meryam said.

"Actually, the question is about *you*."

"I see," Meryam paused, uneasy.

"Why did you want to meet with the Flow? Back in the Bent Tree Clearing?"

Meryam shuffled her feet uncomfortably.

"Well, I didn't *want* to meet with the Flow...but Sarnal forced my hand."

"What do you mean?" Joslyn asked.

"He sent me an anonymous invitation to that meeting spot and told me to bring the stone. Because he said that was the only way to find my...brother... again."

"Your brother?"

"Yes, my brother has been missing for many years," Meryam said. "Sarnal claimed that the only way to get him back was to bring that stone to the Clearing – a 'Reathstone,' as I know now."

"Sorry to hear about your brother..." Joslyn trailed off. Empathy was not her strongest suit. "But...are you saying that you believed an anonymous note asking you to bring a valuable stone to an isolated spot? You thought there was nothing suspicious about that?"

"I had *no other* leads!" Meryam exclaimed. "And I had no idea that you and the others would show up at the *exact* same time and that our stones would all... activate, or whatever, and we would fall through to this place."

"Yeah, but maybe Sarnal did. I mean, making deals with Flow wolves is not the best way to fix problems," Joslyn thought aloud, then immediately regretted the "aloud" part.

"Have you ever lost someone?" Meryam asked, trying to avoid being too defensive.

"Can't say I have ever lost a sibling, no," Joslyn said. "Or a parent either, for that matter. I was orphaned very young. And, hey, that's fine with me. I just learned at an early age how to work alone – to depend on myself, not other people."

"Sounds lonely," Meryam said.

"Well, the good thing about that is..." Joslyn paused a moment, thinking about how to end this sentence, and finally said, "...I wouldn't know."

"There," Meryam said, pointing into the sky. "I think I see one! One of those threads you mentioned!"

Joslyn looked up. "I don't see it," she said, but then remembered her conversation with the sloth back at the river. Apparently not everybody saw the threads when they appeared.

"But if *you* do, it's worth checking out. Maybe it will help us figure out how to get through this chain-link fence."

"It seems to be going in that direction," Meryam pointed north and took a few steps. "But it also is stretching in that direction..." She took a few steps to the south. "Wait, where did it go?"

"Got it." Joslyn was getting the hang of these threads. "We go north, then."

After they had walked a fair distance through the grass along the fence, they came to a small hole. As opposed to the work of the groundhog Joslyn had seen earlier, this new hole was clearly *not* the work of an expert hole digger. It just looked like a poor attempt by some animal to escape from the other side. But fortunately, due to their relatively smaller size, they were just able to fit through it to get into the yard.

As they emerged from the hole under the fence, they assessed their new surroundings.

Ahead of them was a palace made for giants.

Or, rather, it looked like that to our lady adventurers. It was a very rectangular – and angular in general – building of enormous scale. Around the yard they were now in, there were several objects made of wood and brightly colored material, and in the center, there was a large structure with swings attached, all connected to an enormous chute.

"That looks a lot like the transports they use at the mineral refineries in Aponna," Joslyn said, "just ten times larger."

"Actually, to me, it looks more like a *playground*," Meryam observed. "I believe a child lives here."

"Well, if that's true, then it would have to be a *very large* child," Joslyn wondered.

Cautiously, they set off across the yard.

The Chapter with the Cellar Door

"**S**O WE ARE MEANT TO GO OUT OF *THIS* DOOR?**"** Severt wondered, echoing all of the others' sentiments as well.

They all gazed up at the doorknob that was way out of their reach. Without a ladder or something else to climb on, they would not be able to grasp the doorknob, much less turn it to open the door.

"Here! Give me a hand," said Stryton while running over toward a stick-cane-looking object in the corner. Together, they were just able to pull the large stick object to the floor in front of the door.

"Now what?" Freightfurt asked, worried about the noise they were making. It wasn't very loud, but it wouldn't take much noise to alert nearby dogs. Or wolves, for that matter.

"Stand back," Stryton said while motioning them to do just that. Then he leaned on a button at the end of the stick they had just placed in front of the door.

It made a loud "click," and the other end of the stick immediately expanded into a dome, lifting itself off the floor. One side of the dome was resting on the floor, and the other had expanded to reach the doorknob! The team realized that the object that had just expanded was a giant umbrella.

Severt, taking his cue from Stryton, scrambled up the dome and leapt off the top, grabbing the doorknob. He gave it a quick wrench to the side and then fell back on the dome, sliding gently down to the floor again. The company felt a sense of satisfaction as they noticed the huge door had cracked open slightly, thanks to Severt's acrobatic effort.

This satisfaction quickly faded though as they heard the scrambling of furry paws on a floor in a neighboring room and deeper bear-sounding roars similar to what they had heard earlier.

"Oh, my!" said Freightfurt. "That sounds like it could be the Sally's mother!"

"We had best be out the door, and quickly," Severt assessed.

"I'm afraid so," Stryton said. "Sally's mother is a kind person, but she *would* have some difficulty under-standing small stuffed animals that talk and move about on their own. It would spook her, I'm afraid."

"How exactly *have* you managed to coexist with the humans so well?" Shadmack asked.

116

"I just play along, kind of like you did earlier," he said with a smile. He opened the door a little further and motioned for them to leave.

"You'll need to head to the storm cellar in the backyard. I think your little friend's thread will lead you there."

"Also, before I forget..." Stryton continued, turning to Shadmack. "Here, professor. It's yours." The raccoon handed Shadmack the fake book with the Reathstone in it. It glowed brightly as Shadmack accepted it. "Take it with you, and find the others."

Shadmack, Severt, and Freightfurt realized that Stryton intended to stay in the Sally house.

"So you won't be coming home with us, then?" Shadmack asked again.

"Sally needs me," Stryton said with a thoughtful smile. He took a few wistful glances around the foyer they were standing in. "This is my home now."

As they walked through the grass, circling the house, Severt turned to Shadmack and Freightfurt.

"I clearly misjudged our raccoon host in the house earlier," Severt confessed. "He was no enemy at all. But, rather, he was a friend."

"I'm sure he's going to be fine," Shadmack noted. "He's friends with Sally and all of her family, including the dog. He said that Sally adopted him after her dad went away and considers him her favorite toy."

"I certainly hope so, my good badger," Severt said, placing a hand on Shadmack's shoulder.

The squirrel rubbed his paws together. "So, let's assess our situation. You have a Reathstone, as do I. That's two." He indicated the three of them. "If we find one in the cellar, we will have a third, presumably for Freightfurt." Freightfurt performed a little salute. "We will still be in need of two more stones and, of course, the ladies to go with them."

"Nicely summarized," Shadmack complimented. "There doesn't seem to be any better options than to follow your thread again."

"Actually, I can't see this one," Severt said. "But I know from my previous experience to trust Freightfurt when he says that he sees one."

"Experience I do not have, unfortunately," Shadmack sighed.

"Cheer up, my learned friend," Severt said. "We shall find Joslyn and Meryam soon enough. In the meantime, let us see where Freightfurt's thread leads us. I am sure it won't be long before we will need *your* knowledge to supplement *our* directions. After all, when we find all of these...Reathstones..." he held up his own glowing stone from out of his pocket, "...we will need you to help us figure out how to use them."

Freightfurt, following the direction of his thread, led them to a pair of doors in the ground. The doors were almost horizontal to the ground, angled up only slightly. They examined the edges of the door for some sort of hole and were not able to find one.

"Solidly made," Shadmack observed.

"They would have to be of a sturdy build, if they are meant to withstand violent storms," said Severt while they clambered over to the latch that held the door shut.

Here, they had the opposite problem from the front door puzzle they had encountered earlier; they could easily reach the latch, but the three small animals did not have the strength to lift the doors made for giants.

But what if we just removed the latch completely? Shadmack thought. He looked around the latch and noticed there were six screws holding it in place.

"Severt," he motioned to the squirrel. "Do you think we could remove these screws?"

"Possibly." Severt hefted a knife. "What is the objective in so doing?"

"If we remove the whole latch piece, perhaps there will be a hole large enough to squeeze through."

"I catch your meaning," Severt responded. "But the hole would probably be very small. Plus, there are…" he paused while counting, "…six screws here, and I just have one knife to turn them with. It could take some time."

"Not if there are *two* of us doing it," they heard Joslyn's voice say from behind them.

119

The three fellows turned to find their two missing lady companions arriving at the foot of the storm cellar door.

"Huzzah!" Severt exclaimed.

He ran and knelt before Meryam, taking her hand and kissing it. "I feared the worst!"

Severt hurriedly composed himself and then extended a hand to Joslyn, which she half-heartedly shook.

"Yes, your help would be most appreciated, madam," he said to her, answering her earlier question about helping with the screws in the door latch.

"Well, we better get to it, then, loverboy. We got a storm brewin'," Joslyn said, pointing to a dark cloud to their east.

She and Severt set to work, turning the screws as best they could on the latch mount. It was slow work, and the others grew impatient as they saw that the dark cloud had now been joined by a few others just like it.

While turning her screw, Joslyn noticed that Severt's pouch was glowing. "You have a firefly in there or something?"

"It's another Reathstone, actually. We found it in the house," he said. "And its twin is inside this cellar. Or so we think."

"That's good news," she replied, removing the screw and starting to work on another. "With Meryam's red one, that's two down, and...three to go?"

"Actually, we *already* have three," Severt said, still working on his first screw. "Shadmack has one now as well."

"Ah, so if there is one in the cellar, we will have four out of the five," Joslyn assessed, starting on another screw. "That's pretty good progress. Just leaves me or the mouse without one. Do you know where the last one is, after we get this one out of the cellar?"

"I'm afraid not," Severt said as he finished his screw.

"Not to rush you two," Shadmack rushed, "but soon we may need that cellar ourselves for shelter." He gestured toward the darkening skies.

"Don't fret, my good badger. I have completed my toil with this one. A small but worthy foe," Severt said, holding up the screw. "I fear my wrist will be sore in the morning," he said while rubbing it. "So, where is the next...one...?" Severt started to ask but then noticed that while he had been working on his one screw, Joslyn had already finished with the other five screws, and the latch was now completely disconnected.

"All done, then," Severt said. "Brilliant."

Together, they all pulled the latch and its mount out of the door.

A wave of discouragement then hit them when they realized that the resulting hole was still filled with gears and locking mechanisms and things, leaving still too small of an opening for them to fit through. They all peered through it and could barely make out a dark stairway beyond it, descending into darkness.

121

"A setback, to be sure," said Severt, sitting back. "Perhaps there is another way in. We can spread out, investigate that door we came in originally, maybe find another vent..."

Freightfurt tuned out the rest of Severt's sentence as he examined the hole.

He realized it was too small of an opening for all except one of them to fit through.

"I can fit," the mouse spoke up, to the others' surprise.

They all looked at each other and then back at Freightfurt.

Joslyn turned slightly and leaned over toward Shadmack. "I don't think it's a good idea," she muttered under her breath. "That poor guy would faint if he just saw a slightly larger *mouse* in there."

"Freightfurt, I would not ask..." Severt started.

"*You* don't have to ask," Freightfurt said to Severt. "The *thread* is."

"Wait, you guys been seeing those things too?" Joslyn asked. "The weird translucent strings?"

"Yes," Shadmack nodded, pensive. "Almost all of us."

"Can anyone, except Freightfurt, spot any other threads?" Severt asked. None did.

"Just me," Freightfurt said, walking up to the hole. "It's *my* thread. So *I'm* going in."

Severt kneeled down beside Freightfurt and pulled the "T" gem out of the bag. It glowed in his hands. "Remember, it will look like this."

Joslyn walked over to the hole and lowered a rope down through the opening. She, Meryam, Shadmack, and Severt grasped it.

Severt placed a hand on the mouse's shoulder. "Be careful, Freightfurt."

Freightfurt nodded, took the rope, and squeezed through the hole. They lowered him down into the cellar.

The Chapter with the Anticipation

BACK IN THE WORLD OF APONNA, IN THE BLUE Mountains, Sarnal stared at the square pearl. He refused to call it a "Squearl."

He paced the room and considered his future conquest. It was like savoring an upcoming meal. Which of the Cluster Villages would be best to invade first?

Arrant Village would be the most difficult, considering it was full of those pesky archers. Then, they could work from there, village by village. The disarmed soldiers would make great slaves. And with the help of the new Flow arrivals from the Other Side, along with a few allies from the north, their victory would be assured. And he would be King over all.

It is hard to be patient when one's destiny is so clear, he thought.

"My Grace!" Corspar's reptile voice interrupted his thought.

"What is it?!" he snapped, irritated.

"Look! It's turning!" he ran up to the pearl sitting on a podium and jumped up and down in front of it.

The Squearl was red. Sarnal smiled.

"Assemble the team," he told his guards. "It's go time."

The Chapter with the Bravery

FREIGHTFURT SET ONE FOOT ON THE TOP STAIR of the cellar, followed by his other foot. He then let go of the rope. The stairs were large, and he could not see very far into the cellar. He blinked and tried, through sheer force of will, to make his eyes adjust quicker to the sudden change in lighting. The cellar seemed very quiet in general, with just a small hum from time to time that raised and lowered, presumably from some of the machinery used in the giant Sally house above him.

Considering that the stairs were much taller than he was, it was going to take a lot of hanging and dropping to get to the bottom. But the thread had another idea; it led over to the side of the stairs to a railing.

Due to the slope of the cellar opening and stairway, Freightfurt was able to jump on top of the railing. He was startled to find that it was very slick, and without being able to find a way to hold on with his paws, he slid very quickly all the way down the railing and landed in a crumpled heap on the cellar floor.

He looked up and noticed that he was sitting next to a shelf that extended very high up to the ceiling. On the shelf, there were all types of food; he recognized a bag of potatoes here, a box of cereal there. His stomach rumbled. He had been so busy he had forgotten how hungry he was. The Puff Cheese he had eaten earlier had already worn off. He had skipped lunch, and it was now almost time for dinner.

He found one of the legs of the shelf and was encouraged to find there were holes in it. The holes were obviously meant for screws or attachments of some kind, but he was glad to find that he could use them as a ladder. He climbed up to the first shelf and looked around in the dim light.

Immediately in front of him was a large selection of what were clearly toys. Old dolls that looked like miniature versions of the humans, some stuffed animals (that looked very similar to how he did in his current Earth form), and some toy jewelry. One particular piece of this jewelry glowed slightly, and as he walked over to it, it glowed brighter. A stone was inset inside of an earring setting, and carved into the face of the stone was the letter 'H.'

The Reathstone! He picked it up, and a very satisfying full-on glow emanated from the stone. It was different from the other stones they had seen; instead of glowing with a single color, it strobed through all of the colors of the rainbow. One moment it was red, but if he looked away and back again, it was orange, then yellow, etc. He carried it over to the edge of the shelf, and there he froze as it illuminated the rest of the cellar.

For as far as he could see in every direction there were tattered, stuffed, black-furred wolves growling.[16]

Freightfurt, frozen in fear, examined the mass of thrumming wolves below him, their damp, black fur eerily reflecting back the cycling spectrum of light emanating from his newly acquired Reathstone.

The old Freightfurt would have fainted flat on his back, but not this one. Fear was still present though, and it manifested in Freightfurt being frozen on the spot, not able to move even a whisker.

He swallowed once. Twice.

Unfortunately, in his lack of reaction, he didn't consider until too late that while his glowing Reathstone helped him see the wolves, it also allowed them to easily see him.

Freightfurt locked eyes with one of the wolves. He was a little larger than the others, and Freightfurt immediately recognized him. It was the leader they had met upstairs in the house: Gronnal.

Gronnal let loose a loud whistle.

"There he is, boys!" exclaimed the wolf. "He has the prize. And whadaya know?" he asked, looking around the room strobing with light. "He got it to work!

---

[16] This was the source of the hum he had heard earlier. Don't be too critical of Freightfurt's thinking the hum was some kind of Earth machine though. Have you ever heard a hundred or so stuffed animals growling at the same time in an enclosed space? I didn't think so.

Looks like we're going *home, sweet, home*." He said this last with a toothy grin that didn't look so sweet to Freightfurt.

Then Freightfurt startled as an arrow slammed into the shelf wall next to his head. *What?!* he thought. Were the wolves shooting at him now? Had the thread led him to certain death?

But as he looked at the arrow, a wave of familiarity hit him as he remembered his many sessions of target practice with Severt. He recognized that the arrow *was* one of Severt's!

Two ropes extended away from the arrow, one tied to the arrow itself and the other to what looked like a makeshift saddle created from latch parts. Both ropes led all the way back to the tiny hole Freightfurt had originally squeezed through to get into the cellar. He saw Severt's head peering through the hole.

"Quickly!! Hop on, Freightfurt!!" Severt shouted.

The mouse slapped himself across the face and steeled his newfound resolve. He buckled the rainbow Reathstone into his satchel, hopped onto the saddle, and was whisked away as what seemed like a tidal wave of dark fur streamed toward him.

Freightfurt could tell that all four of his companions outside the cellar were hoisting the rope he was holding as fast as they could. But he wished they could hoist faster.

He was now halfway up the stairs and was horrified when the saddle suddenly rotated around its rope, leaving Freightfurt hanging upside down, his bag hanging low toward the wolves chasing him. He gasped at his predicament as some of the wolves started leaping up, gnashing their teeth at him. One of them snagged on his pack, and he felt a piece of it tear off.

With one last tug, Freightfurt made it to the opening and popped through, pulling the bag with the Reathstone behind him. Severt let go of the rope, and it fell into the mass of wolves.

The hole that Freightfurt had just exited was instantly filled with one grungy snout after another, growling and spitting at their just-escaped prey. Large balls of stuffing puffed out of the hole into the night air as the wolves slammed into each other, trying to reach the mouse and his companions. Then the cellar doors started buckling from the mass of wolves slamming into it from below.

"Look! There's a building across the yard!" Joslyn yelled over a loud peal of thunder. Large raindrops started to splatter down all around them.

Together, they all ran to the relatively smaller building Joslyn had pointed out in the corner of the yard, circumventing the swing assembly the girls had seen earlier when they had first arrived.

The building appeared to be a shed of some sort. Behind them, they could hear the remaining pieces of the cellar latch coming apart before the onslaught of the wolves.

As they reached the shed, they were thankful to see the door was cracked open. They ran inside as the rain started falling fast, thundering down on the metal roof above them.

All along the walls on the interior of the shed were objects that seemed like either weapons of war or farming implements. It was difficult to tell, again mainly because of the large size.

Across from them in the shed was a cabinet of some sort, and it was starting to pulse in tandem with the Reathstones they were carrying.

They heard a loud crash outside and knew it was the cellar doors. The wolves had broken out of the cellar and would soon be joining them in the shed.

"We are still missing a Reathstone," Shadmack said. He pointed at the glowing cabinet. "I sure hope it's in there."

"Wait, what's this?" Joslyn said.

She ran over to a bag tied with a bow sitting at the foot of the cabinet. She untied it, revealing a glowing amethyst stone with the letter "A" on it. There were also five lollipops and a piece of paper with a scribbled note. It said:

"HAVE A NICE TRIP!
SPEEDILY YOURS,
-M."

Joslyn hefted the emerald Reathstone. "Yep, that'll work."

Across the Divide, Sarnal paced in front of the Stone Rhombus in the Bent Tree Clearing, the same place where the party of adventurers had vanished. Behind him, two dozen wolves waited with him to greet their long lost brothers.

Tonight, they would feast. And tomorrow, triumph.

The Chapter with the Epiphany

J OSLYN AND SEVERT STEPPED BACK FROM THE provisional door brace they had fashioned out of a few of the unusual tools that were lying around. It would not buy them much time. If they were to leave this strange land of Earth, they had better do so quickly, or else they were going to be doing it with a lot of company.

"Your call, Mack," Joslyn said. "And tell us quickly, if you don't mind. We're about to be neck-deep in wolf."

Shadmack remembered the inscription on the map that pointed to the stones, saying they should be "close set." With this in mind, he announced, "Everyone! Bring your stones over here! Let us put them together."

They all stood in a circle and held out their five Reathstones, edges touching. They still glowed, but no brighter.

Shadmack thought again about the ancient writing. Instead of "close set," a better reading of what it said might be...

"*Closet*!" he exclaimed. "Everyone, bring your Reathstones and stand in a line in front of the closet right over here," Shadmack directed.

They assembled in front of the still-glowing cabinet in a line, facing it. Nothing new happened.

"Now what?" said Meryam.

"Okay – er, line up *single file* facing the cabinet!"

They did so. Still nothing.

They began to hear wolf claws scraping on the shed door.

"Oh yes! Of course!" he exclaimed. "We need to stand in a very specific order and spell the word 'Reath.' They are '*Reath*stones' after all... Meryam – you go first."

They swiftly assembled in order, standing in line so their Reathstones spelled R-E-A-T-H. Nothing continued to happen.

The scratching on the outside had extended to the walls on either side and around to the back.

Shadmack was furiously processing all of the knowledge he had gained from studying the various lore surrounding Reath.

Of course! He had determined that Reath was actually Earth. Perhaps the Reathstones should be used to spell "EARTH" instead!

"Quickly, let's change the order...and spell 'EARTH!'"

They swiftly took their places, standing in a line in order from front to back, this time with Shadmack in first place with his "E" directly in front of the cabinet. Joslyn stepped into the next spot with her "A." Meryam carried her "R" over to the third spot, followed by Severt with a "T" and Freightfurt bringing up the rear furthest from the cabinet with his letter "H."

Now they had lined up to spell E-A-R-T-H...but to no avail. The cabinet was still glowing, but just barely. It seemed to even be fading slightly. They looked quizzically at Shadmack.

There they stood, waiting for the portal to open, and it would not.

"Um, Mack?" Joslyn asked. "Any ideas?"

He shook his head; the din of the scratching wolves was not conducive to formulating solutions.

Suddenly, it occurred to Severt what was out of place.

"Wait. We are going about this wrong," he said.

He turned around and faced his mouse companion standing behind him. "Freightfurt should go first."

Shadmack sputtered, "That can't be right. None of my studies indicate that we should spell anything but 'Reath,' or possibly 'Earth.' If you take the 'H' off the end of E-A-R-T-H and move it to the *front* of the word..." He paused, realizing what the result would be. "Oh, I see."

"Precisely." Severt placed his paw on Freightfurt's shoulder.

"Dear friend. You have served me well for a long time," he said to the little mouse. "And you have also served our company well on our journey. May I humbly request you do so again, and lead us all through?"

Freightfurt nodded, button eyes glistening as he met all of their gazes. They stepped out of the way so that he could move forward from the last place and take his spot at the front. The letters on all of their stones immediately lit up, spelling a much better word, and the only thing that can lead any of us home.

The interior of the shed instantly exploded in color as the cabinet doors flew open. Freightfurt immediately dashed inside with the rest of them following.

Behind them, the doors to the shed gave way to the army of wolves, and they flowed into the room, Gronnal leading the charge. But the only sight the wolves were afforded was Severt tipping his hat to them as he backed into the cabinet.

"Cheerio!" he said and vanished.

Gronnal and his minions were once again stranded on Earth.

The Chapter with the Cabinet

For the first few steps, they were maneuvering around various tools and fabrics hanging above them. But before they had gone many more, they realized that they were now making their way through tree branches instead of tools – first curved branches, then straight ones, until they found themselves in the Blue Mountains of Aponna, in the Bent Tree Clearing. They had changed back to their natural forms also, with real fur, skin, and claws.

But, unfortunately, Sarnal and his guard wolves were there too.

While our adventurers were glad they had fended off an army of wolves on Earth, a dozen wolves still outnumbered the five of them. And they were now facing captivity again. Or worse.

Sarnal growled. "Where is *my brother*?!" he snapped.

"Where is mine?!" Meryam shouted back.

"Guards!" he cried out. "Seize them *and the Reathstones.*" The Flow started to walk forward to do this but were forced to stop as a hail of arrows slashed into the ground in front of them.

Behind Severt and the others, dozens of archers dressed in similar garb to Severt stepped out from behind the trees.

"The Archer-Knights of Arrant!" Severt exclaimed happily. "Brothers and sisters, you are a most welcome sight!" They all nodded and notched their next arrows.

The knight nearest the group smiled. "You aren't the only one doing recon around here, you know, Severt."

Severt turned back to Sarnal.

"That first shot was just a warning. The second will not be."

Outnumbered, Sarnal sneered, turned with all of his company, and fled from the clearing back in the direction of Flow territory.

The Ending

U PON ARRIVING BACK AT THEIR VILLAGES, OUR group of animal friends enjoyed the sort of homecoming that heroes deserve in stories such as these.

Freightfurt decided that he would learn archery, rather than just be the target, for a change. Shadmack had new material for the upcoming art and history festival, which meant that Joslyn would get paid after all. Severt would celebrate with his comrades-in-arms. And Meryam's resolve to find her missing sibling was stronger than ever.

Did they have any further adventures? Of course! But that would take far too long to go into now because... well, it's way past my bedtime. And it's probably past yours as well.

Remember: Each morning can bring new threads. You'll need to get some rest if you're going to follow them.

About the Author

D.L. CRAWFORD GREW UP IN THE DEEP South. Now he lives...Further South. He resides there with a cat that doesn't talk, and his wife and kids, who do.

When he is not writing, he is playing piano, hanging out with family, or planning his next adventure.

CPSIA information can be obtained
at www.ICGtesting.com
Printed in the USA
LVHW042248200120
644180LV00014B/859